Chocolate's
SEVENTH DAY
Soliloquy Vol. 2

S. S. Suggs

Notes by Virgie, Inc.

ISBN: 978-1-7369682-1-5

Cover design by: Art Painter

Printed in the United States of America

Table of Content

Dedication...

This book is dedicated to all of the women seeking love. I have heard from your hearts. And I have etched your answers in my mind. I thank you for taking a chance with me and trying to love differently. I am you and you are Virgie. Stay along for the ride, we are definitely going places.

Love is a challenge that we all are trying to conquer. (Kweisi Gharreau)
Now that's LOVE...

Love Shared...

I want to thank the only little lady who keeps me on my toes. My love for you can't be described. You love your mother and she definitely love you beyond written words.

To J. L., thank you for all you continue to do. You have taken my words to the heart of others and for that I am eternally grateful.

To MJ (even though, you are not the character in the book), I thank you for your prayers, encouragement and support through it all.

To "the rockstar promoter, supporter, and go getter," Shakeela, thank you for all you have done. Thank you for all you're doing and will do in the future. You have gone beyond anything I can ask and need in this process. We are on our way and pat yourself on the back for a job well done. But know, we are not finished yet. I love you with all of my heart, you "Virgie Girl!"

Foreword...

Chocolate's Seventh Day Soliloquy Volume 1 is truly a must read every woman and man can relate to.

The novel is truly exciting, hilarious, real, and compassionate. S. S. Suggs really has her own unique way she connected with her readers through the beautiful touches she puts on each and every page. Oftentimes as I would read the novel, I found myself bursting out in laughter hesitating to put such a captivating book down.

Volume 1 is written in a literal form. But the way S. S. Suggs wrote it seemed like I was watching a high-definition movie. Every scene was so vividly clear and intriguing. I truly connected with that book on so many levels and I bestow all the honor to the author S. S. Suggs.

I saw myself in many of the characters and was literally able to reflect upon myself regarding my own personal experiences with love. Volume 1 described so many moments in the book where I had to stop and think of my own experiences in relationships.

I stand firmly encouraging all mature adults to read the first volume. Volume 1 is just that real. It comes to life from every page of the book and makes you think. There were so many emotions I felt while reading it. I'm beyond excited for Volume 2 to see what's next between the two lovebirds Virgie and her honorable Noble. Their love story is unmatched.

A believer in love,

T. G. Balentine, M.S.
Master's in psychology

Introduction...

I long for the time when we are together again.
When I can see your face inches away from my fingertips.
I reach out my hand to you as an effort to touch you where you stand.
I trail my fingers along your jaw line.

Feeling the softness of your skin against mine.
I recall as I lean into your embrace
I inhale the fragrance of your cologne.
The thought of how delightful the smell of it was
Still makes me aroused.

Aroused...
That I may hang on the smell of its aroma.
As your cologne lingers in my nostrils
I long to touch the fabric closest to your skin.
I long to kiss your lips
Sucking your bottom lip
Then pulling on your top...

The relationship between Virgie and Noble heated up in volume one. They discover what they needed to keep their relationship full of passion and love. This discovery was not without a heart wrenching revelation about the man Virgie has come to love. Noble is a strong black man who appears to have it all together. Virgie is an independent black woman who knows what she likes and needs in her life. Nevertheless, she must acknowledge that she has no idea, who is Noble Winston.

Volume two will journey through the layers that encompasses her man Noble. It will allow us to peel back those layers that are hiding what is in his heart and the things he hasn't share with his woman. We will lose ourselves in the sensual encounters of their intimacy again. And we will continue to witness this couple spark their flame of a loving conversation between a man and his woman.

SUNDAY

I'm lying here holding Mr. Noble in my arms. I never saw this revelation coming. Noble is crying his poor eyes out. He cried all night.

My strong, loving, heartbroken, emotional, and full of regret black man. I wish I knew the right words to say to him to ease that pain in his heart. Noble has been hurting like this for so long. Can the pain he feels be mended? Can he ever overcome this broken heart? Is this the reason Jon thought he would never love again? Has he truly moved on? Do I remind him of her? This man...loving, caring, and affectionate man.

I'm still in awe about what Noble shared. This story is so sad. I empathize with the emptiness he is feeling. My heart hurts for him. I now understand why he wanted to tell me on his own terms. I can't help but cry for him, her, and her family. He really loved her. She really loved him. I can't imagine how my family would cope without me. Noble looks so sad, vulnerable, and broken-hearted. It explains why he is so protective of me, the time we share, and our chocolate soliloquies. He doesn't want to take a moment for granted because time waits for no one.

I recall when a friend of mine told me about what it means to love. He pointed out that there are no guarantees in love, but there will be chances for the opportunity to grow from it. Love is an action word. You can only feel it, hear it, and express it. But can you really? This is a question to ask those you love. I know I show true love to those that mean the most to me. Yet, they still end up questioning me and my love. Actually, I believe love is actually subjective. Love is determined by the person who receives it. It cannot be explained. Love must be felt. When you love someone, it is not with a contentious heart, it is to love with an open heart of understanding. Things will never be perfect. Things will happen but love will allow for those things to change without regret.

Yesterday will forever be a part of our history. I was furious with Noble. Especially, after attorney Sarah McDonald asked Noble those questions about his past. We were in the truck driving away and heading back to his condo.

I was sitting in that truck heavy in thought saying stuff like, "He doesn't love me! Noble has me out here looking like a damn fool. I wondered if Raq and Jon knew what the fuck was going on here because I sure don't have a clue. Of course, they know, they are his closest friends."

I couldn't wait to walk inside his condo. I knew I was going to go the hell off. I am not one of those women who cut up in front of others. But I was going to go the fuck off. He was going to experience my rage. I knew, despite who was around, I would make him a believer. I know I can be quick tempered. Noble's never seen it but that day he was going to discover it. I am not a person he could play games with. I caught a glimpse of him looking all nervous as he sped to his place like he wanted to cry. I said to myself, "Fuck you!" I was so sick of grown ass men acting like teenage boys. I was thinking, "What happened to the days when a man would tell a woman exactly what is happening?"

Who the fuck am I kidding? There was no such day! And, not to mention I remember when men would say within a heartbeat, "man this lady is crazy!" They are the motherfuckers who are driving our bus straight to the hospital. I was so mad! I said, "This man…. this damn man!"

Sunday

The ride took forever. Noble knew if he had driven me home, it would have been over for us, this relationship, and our soliloquies. He wanted to explain himself in the safety of his home. Even as he drove to the condominium, he kept saying "babe please stay calm, babe you know I love you, babe please stay calm, babe you know I love you" over and over again. I was speechless. I wanted to scream, holler, curse him out, punch him in his arm, scratch his face up, I was so angry I felt like I needed to be violent.

At that moment, I understood completely what Twaab did. I wish I had nearly as much confidence or reckless disregard as she had. I suppose that would depend on the person who is judging her actions. I felt like I walked straight into a brick wall. I must've been having an out of body experience. In my mind, I was begging Noble to "drive this truck straight into another one!" This man…this damn man may really be too good to be true. Fuck!

We walked from the garage to the elevator and Noble reached for my hand. I snatched my hand back so hard like "don't you dare touch me!" I could bust a hole in the wall with the amount of force I used to move out of his reach. His face looked bewildered. As, if he didn't know where my anger or hostility was coming from. I was damn mad! I said to myself, "How the hell did he just stand there and let this bitch blind side me with this information?" His stupid ass. He didn't do shit to protect me in that situation. Even though, I'm not sure what he could have done, I definitely feel like he should have done something.

We walked onto the elevator with another couple from the garage. The couple got off on the fourth floor. We would be stuck on this elevator for another nine floors. When the elevator doors closed on the fourth floor, he moved to stand facing me and said, "Babe, please, don't be mad." I was saying to myself, "Really, this some shit!" He was acting like it is not his fault. I was damn mad!

"Then tell me what the fuck is going on Noble?" I put it right back where it should be, with his ass.

"Do you know how difficult it is for me to do this? Tell you about the shame I live with."

"I can't imagine the level of difficulty you are experiencing. Do you know how fucked up this looks? How fucked up I feel? How stupid I looked to my peer? How fucking unbelievable this is playing out for me? How crazy this shit is?"

"I'm sorry for all of this. I never thought I would be standing in the elevator with you discussing my past."

"Noble, you are standing in this elevator avoiding the truth. You haven't said shit. You are dancing around with your answers to my questions. Who the fuck are you Noble Winston? Better yet, do you even know who you are? I have worked with people who have lied for so long that they began believing their own lies. So again, Who the fuck is Dr. Noble Winston? If that is really your name."

"Babe, I am a man…" I interject screaming, "Just tell me goddamn it!" I pushed him out of my face and walked to the front of the elevator. I'm tired of his dancing ass. Dancing around every damn question asked. Afraid of being hit in his ring of lies.

Noble Immediately grabbed my arm. He turned me around to face him and said, "I killed my fiancée!"

This was the last thing I remember happening in that elevator. When I opened my eyes, I realized that I was lying on his couch with a wet towel on my forehead. Those words ringed in my ears, "I killed my fiancée!" These are the words he said to me. The man I love, the man who I want to spend the rest of my life with. Noble is a killer. He killed a woman. Why? Why Noble? Why would you do something so unforgivable? A murderer.

Sunday

A man I thought was soft, sensual, loving, caring, and an adorable human being. But he has a dark side that is filled with anger, aggression, and rage. My Noble was standing over me and I said to him, "Get the fuck away from me!" I jumped up so fast in a defensive stance. I took martial arts as a child. So, I was ready to fuck him up if he was trying to hurt me.

"Are you trying to kill me too?" I said as I moved my hands in front of my body to protect myself. Noble stood there laughing at me. I wasn't playing I was about to kick his ass.

He then said between laughs, "Babe no, I love you! Baby, are you ok?" He continued to laugh like it was a joke. I was dead serious. I didn't think this was a joking matter. He killed his fiancé and now he is probably trying to kill me.

"Babe, you passed out in the elevator I carried you inside. Talk to me!" But his ass, was still laughing.

Damn, I fainted. I thought to myself that this relationship is beginning to be too much. I started crying. This man, this man I'm in love with… he's a murderer. He admitted to me, a civil attorney, that he committed murder. I am an officer of the court.

Why would he burden me with this information? I can't keep this information to myself. There is no privilege here and he is not protected by law disclosing this shit to me. What have I done with my life? My career? My family? My heart? How can I help him? I need to get the hell out of here. I pray he doesn't try to make me stay. Why? Why couldn't this relationship be different? Why did I have to fall for a murderer? He was just sitting on the couch looking at me, sadness in his eyes. I kept telling myself that I needed to get out of his place, leave right at that moment. So, I walked towards the door. I didn't leave I stopped when I heard him cry. I never heard that sound of despair before. Definitely, not from him. My heart broke for him. I walked back to the couch where he was to console him.

Noble continued crying! We sat there sobbing together. Noble said, "Baby I didn't actually kill her, but I blame myself for her death. My whole life is committed to saving lives. The one life that meant the world to me, I didn't save. If I was there, then she would still be alive. She was oil to my skin. I loved everything about her. But something happened and I never discovered what that was. Why Laverne? Why did she leave me?

Laverne was the love of my life. I abandoned her when she needed me the most. She died basically on my watch. Babe, I felt like I didn't deserve to live. How can a doctor allow his patient to doctor on herself? I didn't deserve to practice medicine. When she died, it was as if everything good died inside of me. I just stopped coming around. I didn't go to work. I would not hang out with my guys. I stopped communication with the rest of the world. I would never harm myself, but I had such a feeling of hopelessness behind her death that I disconnected from everything that reminded me of her."

After hearing him say her name from a deep place of love, made me even sadder. I couldn't help but to stretch out my arms to hug him. I have been holding him ever since. We sat there on that couch for hours until both of us had to pee. When he finished, he just went and laid in the bed. I crawled up next to him and wrapped my arms around him. He continued to cry until he fell asleep. This man, this man is the only man I want to love.

I already know on Monday I'm working outside of my office. I am so happy I'm good at what I do. I could have never pulled off working remotely for all of these days. My job is crucial to the financial stability of the company. I'm fortunate enough not to be pressured nor micromanaged to be productive with my cases. They already know "working for wages" is not my thing.

We are preparing for breakfast when Noble says, "This is why I love you so much!"

"Noble, tell me why?"

"Babe, you gave me time and you have every right to have the full story, but you gave me time and you stayed here without judgement."

"I love you too Noble. I gave you the time you needed because I felt the heaviness of what you were holding. So, I needed that to subside first before you were asked to talk."

"Babe, thank you and I'm ready to talk now."

I say to myself "about time" because I'm about to lose it, "Okay I'm listening."

"But let's eat first, I'm starving babe." Damn! But oh well I will wait a little longer because I'm quite hungry too.

He made us breakfast. He cooked turkey bacon, creamy grits, wheat toast with honey butter. We drank cranberry juice. I was washing the dishes when he started talking.

"Laverne was my high school sweetheart. She was a sweet loving young lady. We were the best of friends. I went to medical school and she was a successful businesswoman.We did everything together. I wanted to marry her after our first kiss, but she always said, "a marriage would force everything we have grown to love to change instantly before our eyes."

"She loved our imperfectly perfect relationship. Laverne taught me how to love. When I was a teenager, I was shown what love is. Laverne changed all of that for me."

"Noble, what do you mean differently? Isn't love just that, love?"

"Babe I was taught that kind of love, you know "the love and leave them" type. The men in my life weren't good at treating women like the most important thing in their lives. I made Laverne the most important thing in my life next to my relationship to God. What she needed, wanted, asked, and valued were always provided."

"Noble, what happened? And why do you feel so responsible for her death?"

"Babe, I was working in the ER on July 19, 2017 at 8:14pm. This date and time will forever be imprinted in my mind. I received a call from Laverne saying she wasn't feeling good. She never called because she didn't want to interfere with my job. She became a newly converted vegetarian. She was eating all-natural plant base foods. It never crossed my mind that something was seriously wrong with her. She told me she wasn't feeling good. I told her to lie down, and I would be home soon. Well, "soon" was actually the next day. I didn't call to inform her I would be staying at the hospital. But when I got home, she was laying in the bed unresponsive. I tried to revive her and to no avail I couldn't. I blamed myself for it.

In the mist of him talking, he started to cry again. He continued to share by saying, "Her sister told me the night of Laverne's death she called her. Laverne told her she wasn't feeling good. She told her how I told her to lie down, and that I would be home soon. I later learned she had an allergic reaction to something she ate. We did not know she went into septic shock and died because of it. She would be alive right now had I not told her to lie down. I never even asked her what her symptoms were. I should have known it was something serious because she was never sick enough to call me at the hospital."

Noble just stops talking. He is now crying harder, "She was my everything."

"I didn't know it at the time, but she had me listed as her beneficiary for her estate. Because I had taken care of her for most of her life, she saved every dime she had. Her attorney Sarah McDonald, who we saw yesterday, has been trying to make contact with me because not only is there an estate but Laverne left a letter for me in case of her death."

Noble walks over into the kitchen where I am standing and hugs me tightly still crying.

"Babe I was so hopeless that I told everyone who would listen, I did not want to live. I changed my number; I gave our home to her sister and I quit my job. I wanted to die because for me, life without her wasn't worth living."

"Oh, Noble baby, I'm so sorry. How? When? Are you trying to say that I changed that for you?"

Noble starts chuckling while crying and says, "I love you babe, but I had to learn to love myself again. I found you after I found me." I say to myself, "Lady get over it, it's not always about you." For some odd reason, I think that everything does have something to do with me.

Noble takes my hand and leads me to the couch. I take a seat and he lay his head down in my lap as he finishes telling me what happened. "Babe, I never told anyone I would kill myself. I thought I would if I didn't get away from here. The constant reminder of me discovering Laverne's body in our bed became too much. The constant barrages of calls, questions, and inquiries of how I was doing. I felt like everyone knew that Laverne was gone. And then, everyone knew I was alone. My high school sweetheart, my first love, my confidante, my dearest friend was gone. I made up my mind to leave this place, these people, the reminders, and everything that symbolized us as one. So, I flew to Rome, Italy after her memorial services. Laverne and I promised to go on vacation there that year. We gathered several brochures of the places we would visit. Where we would eat, stay and even the places where we would make love.

Even though I needed to escape here, in my mind I was running into her arms there. I know it may sound crazy, but I needed to be alone with the beautiful images I had of Laverne. I made sure I did everything we had planned to do then I did everything I wanted to do. I ended up staying there for two years. I travelled through Italy as a tourist. I needed to discover what made me happy and not what made us, Laverne and I, happy.

The only person I communicated with during that time away was my sister. Those closest to me contacted her in regard to me. She informed me that while I was gone, surprisingly very few people even inquired about me, my whereabouts, or how I was doing. It was as if I was gone. Laverne always felt like one day she would have to take care of me like I had taken care of her for so many years. I would assure her that we were financially sound. I often told her that she could use her money to do what she liked and allow me to provide for our family. I can assume that she didn't listen and saved it for me. Babe I don't want Laverne's money and I cannot bear to hear her last words written to me."

"Noble, baby maybe you should. You need to move pass the last things you all discussed. Those things that still need an explanation for her death. Why torture yourself with that, those words, and that ultimate outcome? Do you think Laverne would want you burden with this stronghold that engulfs your life?"

"I don't want to talk about it anymore. This is painful to be this exposed. You are the first relationship I had after Laverne's death. I wasn't ready to have this discussion, but I needed you to stay with me. I knew after yesterday's encounter if I didn't, I wouldn't be able to keep you here. I saw the anger in your eyes, and I felt the rage. I never even thought about how I would share this information. I knew I would have to disclose it eventually. My goal was to make you fall helplessly in love with me that you would never want to know."

"Noble, I love you and more than I care to admit. But, at some point in this relationship we will have to discuss your past regardless of how uncomfortable it may be. It is because of my love for you that I will always want to know the story of your

18

past. I would hope that after enjoying your time with yourself that you sought the assistance of a professional. I think you would need to understand why it took this situation to turn things around for you. Are you seeing a therapist?"

"Yes babe, I am. I see a therapist every two weeks for two hours. I have a lot of friends who are therapists. I sought out one who does not know any of us. We have a discussion about my past every session. My therapist believes that my true release to be free will come from my acceptance of my past," while smiling up at me.

"Is your therapist in favor of you starting a new relationship?"

Noble doesn't make a sound and lies there still. After a long pause he says, "My therapist thinks this is a bad decision and that I'm not ready to love again. I don't care what anyone thinks about what I am doing. I have made up my mind to love again. And, I have decided to love you."

I feel like passing out again. I'm speechless!

I'm sitting on this couch rubbing Noble's head thinking about everything he said. I wonder why his therapist doesn't think he is ready to start loving again. Duh, because he is not over her. He can't even go get the letter from Sarah. I wonder how much money she left him. Laverne sounds like she was a beautiful person. I wonder are these soliloquies what he learned from her. Noble is definitely a freak maybe she taught him all these freaky things he loves to do.

I wonder was she neat like him or did it drive her crazy. I want to see a picture of her. Have I met her sister and didn't know who she was at the time? Why did he just tell his little sister where he was going? I wondered if she told anyone. I know why he told her because he was financially responsible for her. She had to know where he was in case, she needed something. What did he do in Rome? Natasha Janine and I went there, and we loved it. How do you quit being a doctor? So, he is not on a leave of absence, he used to be a doctor. How did his mother and her brother feel about him not being able to talk to him? His therapist says he is not ready then why in the hell am I still here. I should leave.

"Noble, I'm going to go home so I can process everything. I need the comfort of my home. Okay?"

"Babe, do you remember me saying that if I start talking about my past that it would affect our relationship?"

"Yes, I remember."

"Virgie, this is why? This is why I said that to you. You are here trying to make sense of it all." Noble sits up then move to the floor. He is facing me as he speaks. I want to run and hide so badly but I stay seated. He knows I shy away from this kind of confrontational conversation. I don't want him to do his Jedi mind trick on me. I need to leave. I want to leave. But I am still sitting right here.

"Virgie, all you need to know is I love you for who you are. I have never compared you to Laverne. She is not here. It is you and me. You are the woman I love but that doesn't mean I stopped loving her. She is a huge part of why I am the man I am. To be perfectly honest, she is why I can love you too. The way you need to be loved."

"Noble, if this is true then why does your therapist feel like you are not ready for love again. Why do you think your therapist doesn't feel like you are ready?"

"Babe, he believes if I can't close my chapter with Laverne by meeting with her attorney, then I am no good for you. And he believes you are not ready for my love because you need therapy too."

"Your therapist said, what? He doesn't even know me, and he has something to say. I don't need therapy. If anyone is taking notes, I'm perfectly fine."

"Babe, you are not ready. Every time something or someone says something that doesn't fit inside of that logical box in your head, you are running to the door. You just said you need to leave to process what I told you. It doesn't fit in your box so now you want to go to either call Natasha Janine or a family member to make it make sense. I want you to stay here even if it doesn't make sense. Stay here with me and let's process it together. Our relationship has to be about us, how we feel about us, and what we do for us. If therapy taught me anything, it's what I feel matters before what others feel about me."

Noble gets up off of the floor and is now on his knees in front of me. I can see the hurt in his eyes and says, "I love loving you and that's what makes sense to me." This man, this man has me crying all over again.

All of that talking and crying gave me a headache. Noble is sleeping like nothing changed. I just don't know what to do but I know I still want every broken piece of him. Yeah, he has some issues, but we all do. He loves me, he makes me laugh, he makes me cry, he holds me when I need to be held, and he meets my emotional needs. He knows exactly when I need to be flattered and spoiled. He is fine, sexy, intelligent, strong, wise beyond his years, rich, and smooth as silk. Nevertheless, he is broken, fearful, an emotional wreck, guarded, protective, and quite secretive.

So, where do I go from here? Do I forget the things I know? Do I press him for answers to my questions? Do I spend my time trying to understand his past? Do I stop trying to make sense of it all? I'm so confused. I know I love him, but I just don't know if that will be enough. I have love men in the past and still I was left heartbroken. I spend so much time guarding my heart that when it beats for love, I will not recognize it.

I thought that Kelle and I would be here right now married with children. When I say I loved that man, I loved that man. He was all I thought about. I would spend long nights in that restaurant doing what I could to help him. I thought that's what was required of me as his girlfriend. I would get up early in the morning to go there just to kiss him before I began my day. It wasn't enough for him or for me. It was our inability to discuss what we needed that made for a hopeless relationship. Noble isn't Kelle. He wants to process it with me. He doesn't want me to leave without it making sense. He needs me here. Here I am still confused by it all. I don't know what to do but what I do know is I love this man right here.

"Babe, you can't sleep. What's wrong?"

"Noble, you know me I will think my way straight into insomnia."

Noble wraps me up in his arms while I just cry into his chest. I feel like I'm loved when I'm in his arms regardless of the complexity his arms hold. He is a complex man who loves hard. I bet Laverne was protective of him too. Who wouldn't be for a man like Noble? After everything that he has said, I still choose him. I even believe that if he had told me he killed her, I would have thought "he had to do that to make room for me." To even think this is crazy. I'm so far gone that I will take this murderous man over a man like Kelle any day because he does it for me. He ignites every wick of a candle in my body. I want all of this man and everything that comes with him.

We are lying in the stillness of the room. I wonder what he is thinking about. I know what I'm thinking about, us. What are we going to do? How can we move on after this? Where do we go from here? I have never felt like this for any man. Noble makes everything in me come alive. He walks into a room and all I want to do is touch him. I want to kiss his full lips. I want to rub my hands over his chest. I want to squeeze his arms. And I want him to do the same thing to me.

MONDAY

It's five o'clock in the morning, well to be exact it's 4:45 a.m. and I am lying here wide awake. He is lying on my chest with his ear to my heart. While he is doing this, he starts telling me what he needs.

"Virgie, can you pull me in closer to you? Babe I want to move to the rhythm of the drum you beat," as he is rubbing my thighs.

"Can I come so close to your body, that our bodies become one," as he pulls me up to kiss my neck.

"Will this pull you possess draw me a map to your heart," as he leans me back on to the couch and begins to kiss my chest.

"I want this pull to bring me down to that spot that makes everything tingle," as he slides his hand down into my shorts.

"Babe I'm talking about the pull that causes the unrest of civility in your body," as he is touching the wetness of my release.

"I need you to let go of everything you have pulled inside of you. I need that pull that can make you forget societal strongholds on what's right and what's wrong."

I'm in a trance from all of the emotions I'm feeling right now. It makes me speechless, so I can't tell him to give me more. But he does anyway.

"The pull that makes everything about this wrong but oh so right," as he is using his fingers as tools to remove whatever needs to come out.

"The pull that breaks all ties and locks that keeps me away from you," as he begins kissing me in my mouth.

"The pull that forces me to miss you when you are here, but far away in your thoughts," as he picks me up and places me on top of him.

23

"The pull that confuses my normalcy, distracts my current, and rattles what is to become of us," as he lifts me up and down on top of his pants so that I can feel the rise of his penis.

"Can I pull you up to meet me where I am, when you fall," as he slides his hands in the back of my shorts squeezing my derrière.

"I want to be all around and through here to pull that thing that hold us back. Please allow me to be the one to pull on you," as he lifts my shirt over my head and sucks on my breast.

He is sucking these breasts like a baby nursing on his mother. He is stroking my back, biting my nipples, and squeezing my derrière. I want all of him right now and right here. I know he needs me. I absolutely love the feeling of being needed. He helps me reach peaks I never envisioned conquering. He is my man. And I now know I am his woman.

Noble crawls over me so that I can be face to face with him because he knows I shy away.

He places his hand on my chest over my heart and says, "Babe, may I dwell in this house to love, cherish and protect you. May I seek your secret spaces that hold your true desires. May I always value your opinions even if I disagree. May the unspoken love I have for you be heard with your heart. May the notes of your heart forever be your song. Babe, will you be my housekeeper?"

I hit him in his chest, "You play way too much. Noble, you had me over here thinking you were about to propose to me."

"Virgie, if you had listened with your heart then you would have known what I did! Babe, you are so use to traditional ways of things happening that you question new approaches to loving someone. Remember when I introduced you to our Chocolate Soliloquies, you thought it was ridiculous. I had to literally beg you to have an open mind and after constantly reminding you of the softness of those encounters, we are now here. Experiencing love differently and without reservation.

"Wait a minute, you what? No, you didn't. Did you just propose to me? Are you serious? No, you still playing. Stop playing and be serious. Noble, say it again."

"Babe, you weren't ready and hopefully you will be next time."

"What? Are you for real? Knock it off, wow! Next time, we'll if it wasn't this time who can say if there will be a next."

"Ms. Lady, there will be a next time you just need to be ready when it happens! Now, let me give you something to help you sleep," as he leads me to the bedroom.

Noble is under these covers making me scream from delight. What is he doing down there? I can't take it. No, he should stop, no he shouldn't stop. "Noble, I can't. Baby, oh baby! Yes, yes. Noble! Oh, oh, oh, you know you. Baby, yes baby, yes. I am, oh I am, I am. That's it, that's it. Oh, that's it, baby! Oh baby, I'm fucked," was the last thing I would say before he comes out from under these sheets, with my bodily juices all over and around his mouth.

He crawls up to me and says, "I need you to taste what I taste," and places his mouth over mine. This is so arousing I am here tasting the sweetness of myself. I begin licking his face taking in every drop of me back into my body.

"Noble, does my tongue have the taste of me?"

"Babe, yes! Hell yes, I love the taste of you!" And then I say, "With every swallow are you aroused and wanting more?"

"Baby, yes hell yes! Talk me through it! This the shit I can't get enough of!"

"Well, I need to release so can you unplug me? Noble, allow me to release in the way you are the most pleased? Tell me what I need to do and don't leave out any details?"

"Babe, turn over and grab a hold of the headboard."

"I am seeking everything you have stocked up inside of this house," he says while smacking my cushion real hard.

"It is at your exit that I will make my entrance. The door has been left open," he says as he uses the small instruments of his hands to touch me. I feel them, thrusting inside of me pushing me forward.

"Babe, hold on and leave your hesitation right at its entrance. I am checking my surroundings because when I enter it will be because I know that this house welcomes me home." And he removes the instruments then to thrust his muscle inside my muscle but this time I'm holding on tight.

He says, "You guide me along my way." So, I push back why he continues to thrust me forward. We are moving to the same beat. Our bodies are moving as one slow then fast then slow and fast again.

"Babe don't release without me."

"Baby, I'm ready," and his pace quickens, and we release everything that we had in us plugged up at the same time.

I jump on top of him placing his muscle back inside my opening.

"This house has done the necessary preparation to be ready for you. A house full of sexy surprises. You feel this large couch perfect for two," as I squeeze the muscle of my vagina. "What about this high countertop, strong enough to hold us up," as I grab my breast moving up and down.

"These walls are stable enough for the weight of this thrust happening against them. It slippery floors that are an ideal method for sliding back and forth," as I'm moving up and down.

"We are walking around it to and from in here. Can you feel this shower powerful enough to soothe this aching muscle and insulated enough to the hold in our noises?" I say as I can feel my body release its juices.

"This house is equipped to handle the passion you will bring. The passion that erupts leaving my soaking wet release. It is a house capable of utilizing my other openings to clean off any other spills," as I am kissing him sucking his tongue. "A house where all of the rooms can be used for your delight," as I am picking up speed riding on top of him.

"You can enter the wide-open space in the back, placing yourself in there," as I say while grabbing my butt. "You will need to move around because you are seeking to get a feel of this place. But the warmth of it will captivate you. Are you at a loss for words?" I ask because he hasn't said a word since I have been riding him like a horse.

"The intense expression on your face reveals the pleasure you have. You are touching these walls in this house softly then rubbing them in awe. This is the house where you eat until you are full. You will enjoy your nibbling and biting," as I am reaching my peak of release moving up and down rolling back and forth.

"I will make you tired from all of the explorations of my hidden places. I will expose what they are made to do while handling anything new. This house is where you delight yourself in the simple nuisances of pleasure," as I go faster and faster up and down.

"Baby, I'm so elated that you lay here all the morning long. The temperature of this house is set to hot." And there I am releasing like a fountain, all of my bodily juices going everywhere, talk about being unplugged. I'm so exhausted now so I fall over and fall fast to sleep.

I could hear my cellphone buzzing. It feels late in the morning but it's only 7:19 a.m. I remember it is in my pants pocket over there on the floor. I get up to retrieve it because it continues to vibrate. I pull the phone out of my pocket and I see that it is my sister MJ calling me.

I answer, "Morning sister what's wrong? Are you serious, sister? My God, I'm on my way. I am at Noble's house. We will be there soon. Love you too sister, be careful. Noble, get up Auntie had a heart attack and is at the hospital."

"Babe, I'm so sorry to hear this. Ok let's get out of here. Are you going to contact your sisters?"

"MJ has already called Twaab, but she hasn't spoken with Dominica. She is at the hospital."

"Babe, let me hop in the shower first."

I'm crying and say, "No let's just go right now."

"Babe, after everything we did this morning, we are not smelling like our freshest selves, I'm not playing babe."

Before I can respond, I bust out laughing. He wasn't wrong so I say, you're right but let's do it quickly. I notice Noble is sitting up in the bed laughing too hard. This man, this man.

Here we are again on our way to the hospital for a family emergency. This time the ride there feels different my aunt is elderly. I'm so sad by this information because she means the world to me. She is the matriarch of our family. We don't do anything without input from her. My sister Twaab always complains that Auntie begs too much, and she is using me. I know she does. I call it an honor to help her because she has helped us when we had nothing. MJ is the sister who really cares for her, so I hurt for her right now. I wonder did all the screwing around with her man do this.

Mr. Sid gave my aunt a heart attack, wow old people be getting it on. Auntie knows she has no business humping around the way she does.

Noble interrupts my thoughts and says, "Babe are you ok? You are pretty quiet over there."

"Yeah, I'm just thinking about Auntie and what may be going on with her." I turn and realize we are now pulling up to the emergency room as we speak.

Noble drops me off at the door. He then leaves to park my car in the garage. As I am walking up to the door, I can see that this visit will not be good. Kelle is standing next to Mr. Sid in the waiting room. I could just die. Why? Why the fuck would Kelle come? First off, he knows this is my aunt so there is no surprise there. He knows I would be here because she means the world to me. He knows damn well he should have his ass at his restaurant. Noble will not like this. This will not be good. Noble is going to go off especially after I told him the shit Kelle said.

I am so focused on Kelle's ass that I didn't see MJ walk up and hug me.

"Sister, are you alright?"

"Sister, what the fuck is Kelle doing here? I can't rid myself from his ass. Fuck!"

"Virgie, he has been here all morning with Sid. You know Sid is like his father. What's wrong with him being here?"

"MJ, everything! Every damn thing. Fuck!"

The next thing I hear is MJ saying, "Hey Noble, how are you? We can't keep hanging out at the hospital, we're going to need to find better places to get acquainted."

He leans into hug MJ and I can see it, he has spotted Kelle ass standing with Mr. Sid.

Noble says to MJ, "Excuse me one moment I need to speak to Virgie!" Here it comes, damn!

He grabs my arm, "What the fuck is he doing here?"

"Babe, he is here with Mr. Sid." I probably should have mentioned this.

"Mr. Sid is my aunt's boyfriend who happens to be the chef at Kelle's restaurant and Kelle's play father. They are really close."

"What the fuck? You knew he would be here? You let me be blindsided with this shit? This motherfucker! I should kick his ass right now! He better be lucky your aunt is sick because I would fuck him up."

"Noble, calm down I told you I checked him."

"Virgie, I will never send nor have a woman to do my job. I can't believe this fucker, yes, I can. I bet it was his damn idea to hook that man up with your aunt."

I'm sitting trying to recall how did it happen and Noble says, "don't be smiling in the fucker's face, I'm not playing."

"Noble, I won't."

"Yeah ok, I know you." He definitely doesn't know Kelle because he will be the person smiling in my damn face. Kelle's ass never learns. And he comes undone when it has something to do with me.

"Whatever!" I can't stand Kelle's ass. He knew I would be here. I say to myself, "This motherfucker is getting on my damn nerve."

We walk through the door and Noble is holding my hand leading me into the waiting area.

Mr. Sid walks up to me and says, "Hey Virgie, I'm so sorry! I promise I will not be taking any more of those damn pills. I don't want to kill my baby. I love Katerina with her crazy ass. I promise, I'm going to result to a normal sex life. She is the one who encouraged me to take them damn things in the first place. You should have seen me always trying to hide because I was sticking out. I told her that I would only take them when I stayed over to her place. I would be so embarrassed to leave my house. I remember that one time I showed up to work with my jacket tied around my waist. But I didn't take them yesterday, so I am so confused by this. And now, we are all at the hospital," and he starts to tear up.

"Mr. Sid, I'm sure she will be ok. I would like for you to meet the man of my life Dr. Noble."

Noble extends his hand and says, "It's just Noble sir."

Within a blink of an eye, here comes Kelle's ass so I grab Noble hand tightly like "be nice." I don't want Noble to act up in here. He used to work here and all he needs is for people to see him act a fool after everything he shared with me. Please let him keep his cool, please!

Kelle extends his hand to Noble and says, "Hello, young man, I'm Kelle of Kelle's restaurant. How do you do?"

Noble says, "I'm quite well, how are you?" Then squeezes me against his body giving Kelle, the "she is mine" stare like he doesn't know it. Kelle is standing up here smiling like, "yeah yours now but I had her first." I felt like a pawn being used for their testosterone pleasure.

Kelle turns to me and says, "How are you Ms. Virgie? I'm sorry to hear about your aunt. I have been here supporting my dad because he has been truly hurt by this."

Before I could respond Noble takes my hand and says, "Let's go check on your aunt, I'm sure you are anxious to see her."

"Ok, thanks babe," as we walk away. I really want to say to him to cut it out and knock this shit off. I decided to keep the peace, so I follow behind him to the receptionist desk.

Noble is talking to the nurse and you can see her ass giggling and batting her eyes. She is twirling her hair like he is so damn funny.

I tap him and when he turns to me. I lean into him and say, "stop smiling in her damn face, I'm not playing either," with my nose flared and eyebrows raised.

He then gives me a kiss and says, "Yes babe, I love you too!" He knows damn well I didn't say I love his ass. He better stop playing with me.

I can see Kelle ass looking stupid. This damn lady happens to be looking stupid too because she caught my expression of displeasure with this shit. I stop that giggling shit immediately. I walk over to talk with MJ who looks so sad and worried leaving Noble at the desk.

"Sister, are you okay?"

"Virgie, Auntie is really sick, and I'm scared," says MJ.

"Let's talk with the doctor first before we start thinking like she can't heal from this. I don't want to worry until they say we need to worry."

Now, here come Kelle's ass again. This man is pissing me off, I wish his ass would go home but he won't.

"MJ are you okay?" Before she could answer I respond, "Kelle, go see about your damn dad. Let me see and worry about my sister!"

Noble hears me and come over and say, "You should take her advice because this is not the time nor place but it can be if you choose not to listen."

Kelle walks back over to Mr. Sid at which time Dr. Tapes comes out into the lobby to greet and give us an update.

Noble greets his friend and Dr. Tapes says, "Your aunt is resting. It appears that she didn't have a heart attack but actually suffered stress cardiomyopathy. Stress cardiomyopathy is similar to heart attack symptoms but are not life threatening. We are running some tests for further evaluation."

MJ says, "Thank you doctor. Are we able to see her?" She is standing here smiling her ass off to the doctor.

"Not at this time but she did ask me to take you to dinner as a favor to her." Auntie is crazy as hell. Why would she tell him that? This old lady is something else.

Noble says, "She asked you what?" Noble obviously doesn't know my Auntie. She has no buffer. I thought he would have figured that out from when he met her. I guess he is slow in that department.

"Yeah dude, she told me that if I didn't take her niece MJ to dinner that she would report me for medical malpractice. So, I told her I need my license." Auntie wouldn't do that. She would never work against someone losing a job. She would report you in a heartbeat then tell them to educate the employee. I saw her one time report a waiter for his rudeness. Then told the manager,

"When I visit your establishment again, I will ask him what he has learned." She did just that when we returned to that restaurant. She made me give him a big tip to make up for the last visit when we didn't. She never brings money when we go out. I think Twaab is right she is using me.

"Doctor don't pay her no mind. I think she is suffering from delirium but I'm not a doctor." MJ is still smiling talking this talk "I'm not a doctor" what the hell.

"She seemed pretty serious, but I don't mind taking a beautiful lady out to dinner." Auntie is serious but wait a minute did he say he will do it. Wow!

MJ turns red. Noble, and I are smiling from ear to ear. MJ should say something. She is standing up here like a deer in headlights. Open your damn mouth girl. I guess I better say it for her.

So, I say, "How about this Wednesday you both can come over to our place for dinner as our guests."

MJ reluctantly refuses initially so I hit her arm and she then agrees. Dr. Tapes agrees without even being prompted to do so.

Mr. Sid was finally allowed to see Auntie, so we had to wait out there with Kelle's ass looking stupid. MJ is still smiling that she is finally going on a date with a fine ass black doctor.

Noble says to Kelle, "I discussed with Virgie how you and I should make some time to have a conversation. She didn't think it would be a good idea. But since you are here, I think this would be the perfect time to do it. What do you think?" Kelle's ass is going to say no. He doesn't want any trouble.

Kelle says, "I would agree. Let's step outside to talk." What the fuck? I didn't see none of that coming. Damn, the one time I wanted his ass to sit down somewhere he gets his ass right on up.

Noble gets up and Kelle follows behind him. I'm thinking to myself why the hell are they doing this. Noble should have let this shit be. I can't believe this.

MJ snaps me back into reality and says, "Why are your boyfriends trying to fight at the hospital? Well at least they don't have far to travel to get patched up. I'm surprised Noble would even consider this. He doesn't look like the type who would be bothered by another man. Now, Kelle is that type of a guy."

"MJ shut the hell up! I can't read lips and listen to your ass." She just starts laughing and gets up and walks away.

From the looks of the interaction with Noble and Kelle through this window, I can see they are definitely arguing. It seems as if Kelle is doing all the talking and Noble is responding every now and again. I am so engrossed with watching them and didn't see Mr. Sid walk up.

"Virgie, where is Kelle?" I want to say that his dumb ass is out there about to get his ass kicked.

"He is outside talking to Noble."

"Well, that's what grown men do when they find themselves loving the same woman. They are not the first men to have a conversation about the woman they both loves. You know in my younger days I was a little player. I had plenty of women. I was slick and smooth. All the ladies loved me. I changed my life when I realized how wrong I was trying to control a woman as she was a piece of property.

I used to have conversations with other players in the hood about who belongs to who. If a lady was my lady, the players knew. She was off limits and the players knew what I was capable of doing if they messed with her too. I can recall one time when there was this man, a young cat, approached me outside my nightclub telling me he wanted one of my red bones (you know that's what we called light skinned ladies back in the day).

Well, let's just say it didn't go well for him. I kicked his ass. I learned in that moment. Even though, he wasn't strong enough to take her from me, he had heart for coming to me as a man about how he felt. It takes a different kind of man to stand up for himself. He didn't know how that would turn out, but he was not going to be deterred. I never gave him one of my redbones, but I did view him differently after that. He took his ass whooping like a man."

I don't know what the hell Mr. Sid is talking about I just don't want Noble to beat Kelle ass at this hospital that's my only concern.

MJ goes to the room to see Auntie, but I am waiting for Noble. Dr. Tapes comes back to the waiting room. "Virgie, where is Noble?" I want to say outside acting like an ass with Kelle.

"He is outside talking to my ex-boyfriend about leaving me alone." We look at each other at the same time and start laughing. At this moment, Noble and Kelle walk back into the waiting room. Kelle walks over to the area where Mr. Sid was sitting while Noble walk towards Jon and myself.

"What's so funny?" Because we were still laughing when he walked over to us.

"You! We were laughing at you out there talking to my ex-boyfriend." He is goofy as hell for this.

"Babe you too old to be talking like you're a young girl with a jealous boyfriend. I was out there talking to a grown man about respect that's it, that's all. Let you tell it, you already talked to your ex-boyfriend about that." I want to go off since he is standing up here being a smart ass but I'm going to keep quiet for now and I mean now.

"Okay I will leave you grown men, to tend to your grown men conversation," as I walk away from him. I hope Noble knows I'm mad as hell but if he doesn't know it, he will real soon.

I was able to see Auntie and she is feeling better which made us all feel better. She is supposed to be discharged today. Mr. Sid will see to her getting home. We are on our way home when I notice Noble make a right turn instead if a left turn towards his condo. While Noble is driving, we both are surprisingly quiet. I am not talking nor is he.

"Noble, what the fuck is your problem?" He has the nerve to be upset and upset with me. Man, bye!

"Excuse me, what do you mean? You were the one standing up there laughing at me with my fucking friend. And, I have a problem. I should be asking you, what the fuck is your problem?"

"Noble, we were just laughing." What is the big deal? He is tripping because we were laughing.

"Virgie, listen to yourself. You were standing up there with my fucking friend laughing at me while I am talking to your disrespectful ass ex-boyfriend. I'm not sure of the men you are used to dating. You know what, I do know, because I was just talking to his ass. That shit wasn't cool. You need to ponder on that. Since you are so curious to know what the fucked is up with me."

I am speechless. He then looks over at me and says, "Do you want me to drive to your house? Because I can get an Uber to take me home, so you don't have to drive."

"If that's what you want to do, it's fine." Really Noble, isn't this some shit.

"Virgie, I want to go home but this is the shit that's too much for me. I refused to be disrespected or humiliated." What? When did I do that? Me? No!

"How did I disrespect you by laughing with your friend?" Now this is interesting. What is he talking about?

"Yeah, I'm going to drive you home and get an Uber." He is going to leave after all the shit he said yesterday. Wow, this is fucked up.

"Okay, fine then drive to my apartment." I'm not going to beg him to stay. This is fucked up but it's what he wants to do.

He pulls in the garage and as we are walking to the elevator Noble is on his phone requesting an Uber.

"Are you leaving now Noble?" Don't leave me. I'm so sorry. I should tell him that. I don't want him to go.

"Yeah, I'm tired!" He is not tired. He is mad there is a difference. I should say something.

"Really Noble, you are mad so you're going to leave but when I'm mad, I stay to get clarity, now that's fucked up."

"Virgie, do you want me to stay?" Hell, yeah, I do. I always want him to stay with me.

"Of course, I do, I don't want you to leave mad. I want to process this with you." I really don't because I don't even get why he is mad. His friend and I was joking around. What is the big deal about that?

"Okay Virgie, I'll cancel my request." Thank you!

I lean in to kiss him. He gives me his cheek instead of letting me kiss his lips. We walk onto the elevator and I am holding his hand when someone says, "Hold the elevator please."

Noble let go of my hand and holds the elevator open. I can't believe my eyes. This bitch Mari and another bitch who I think is Shenine are getting onto the elevator.

"Thank you, sir." This bitch. I want my damn tip back since she played like she didn't know Natasha Janine. She better give it back or I will take it out of her ass. I can't stand her.

And then the lady with Mari says, "Hello Dr. Winston." Yep, this is that Shenine bitch!

"Hey!" Noble didn't give her ass even a wink. I think he is still mad at me so he can't even process.

This bitch Mari says, "Hey Virgie. How is Natasha Janine?"

Before I can swallow my spit, "Bitch don't ever in your damn life ask me questions. Fuck your hey and your hoe," while I mean mugged them both like "say something." I will kick both of their ass right here on this elevator, weak ass links. They don't know me but since Mari wants to play like she does then I will fuck her up right here.

Noble moves in front of me and start kissing me. I cannot even enjoy it because I am mad as hell. She is so lucky the elevator door opens and Noble decides to pick me up and carry me out of that elevator. I want her ass to say something so right before that door closed, I yell, "Bye bitch!" We didn't even make it to my floor yet. Man, I'm mad now we have to wait for another elevator just to get to my apartment.

Noble is standing in the hall shaking his head at me. "What is your problem?"

"Nothing Westside, you had me a little nervous there!" He better recognized I will fuck them up.

"I can't stand her. She knows what the fuck she is doing to Natasha Janine and her career. She keeps wrapping her up in this mess. She is lucky you were on the elevator too. I would have bust her in her face. I was ready for her hoe to jump too."

"Okay, Westside prime fighter, you were going to take them both out with a one two punch."

"You have jokes, but I'm telling you I was about to give it to their ass." Right there in the elevator.

"Now you know how I felt when I saw old boy." What? He felt like fucking Kelle up. I didn't know that at all.

I turn and hug him, "I'm sorry, I love you and would never try to disrespect or humiliate you." I mean what I am saying because he means too much to me for me to do that to him.

"Babe, I know I was caught up in my feelings, but I wanted to hurt that dude. I had to exercise some restraint. And I became furious when I saw you laughing with Jon when I was doing what you asked of me."

"Baby, I didn't even think about it like that, but I understand completely I'm so sorry. Do you forgive me?"

"Yes, I forgive you! Do you know that I love you for real with every part of me? I did something today I would have never done. I had a conversation with a man who is destined to be fucked up by me. His bitch ass is going to stay in my business. I did that for you because I love you just that much!"

"Noble?" Damn, I fucked that up. I lost sight of the big picture. I asked him to be nice and he did that. I should have been more sympathetic of his feeling. It never even crossed my mind.

"Yes babe?" I love to hear him call me "babe." It is something about the way it rolls off of his tongue.

"Can you make love to me?" We are always having some form of freaky sex, but I desire lovemaking. I need that tender touch tonight. Slow, soft, and full of passion kind of sex. Nothing kinky, wild, and unfiltered.

"Of course, I can, will, and always want too," then he kisses and sucks on the nape of my neck. The elevator doors open, and we are so lost in each other's arms. We're standing here holding each other just like the first time we met. This man, this man, this man.

TUESDAY

There was nothing erotic about last night. Noble and I just made love. And that love we made was so emotional, tender, affectionate, full of passion, and loving. We both cried and Noble kept crying. I don't know why he was so emotional, but I think it has something to do with Laverne. I think he is feeling guilty for moving on. I cried because I have never loved anyone like I love him. I love him with my whole heart, and he is the first man I don't want to live without. He makes me happy, and he is happy to make me happy too.

"Babe, why when I wake up, you're always awake in heavy thought? What are you thinking?"

"I'm thinking about how I am going to return to this office today." I want to stay in this bed with my man, but work calls and I must answer.

"You don't have to go, you can always stay with me in my little foreclosure," and we both start laughing.

"I wish I could, but I do need to go into the office today." He always wants to go to his house. He is uneasy about my place ever since that incident occurred. I don't blame him because before I knew Natasha Janine was involved in it. I thought nothing of it. I feel the uneasy feeling because I know all of the parties involved. And how seriously dangerous this incident is.

"Babe, I want to go somewhere this weekend." He wants to take me somewhere. I don't see a problem with that.

"Noble, where do you want to go?" I really wish we could leave now but I have a lot of work I need to do.

"Can I be trusted with the details of our getaway? We need a break and these last couple of weeks have been full of revelations. It will do us good to get away."

"Okay, I will leave it in your hands. I'm going to trust you with the details. You are absolutely correct we need a vacation from here."

"Babe, since you're going to work. I was wondering if I could have some of that wild sexy sex I love. So, every time you feel that slight pinch, you will know I was there."

"Really Noble, after all the love making, we did last night you need some more."

"Babe, it's just that good, I got to have it." He says while lying in this bed with his Duchenne smile.

"Since it's at your request, I'm instantly aroused. Can I just sit on your face and when I'm ready to release you take it all in?" He loves this too. When we first started having relations, he said this is his thing.

"Hell yeah!" I knew it. He would be excited for that. Everyone has a thing.

"But Mr. Noble, you can't use your hands." I'm going to make it harder for him. It won't be easy mister.

"I wouldn't have it any other way." I love he is confident, but I have another request too.

"And blindfolded babe." Let see what you have to say now.

"So, you want to see if I could find my way. Believe me Ms. Lady, I know every piece of tissue, blood vessel, and layer of skin that makes up that muscle. You don't even have to blindfold me. I promise I will keep my eyes closed."

This is what I really love about Noble. He encourages me to be me. Not to mention, he enjoys acting out some of my wildest fantasies. If our role play doesn't work out, then we will tweak it so it will. That's what is so wonderful about him. I've always wanted to do some of these wild erotic things. I never had anyone like him who loves to keep it spicy. And now I have the chance to do whatever, whenever, and however I would like.

41

I'm already at work walking into my office when my receptionist hands me my messages. I have several messages from Natasha Janine and several messages from my clients worried about their cases. I will return the calls of my clients first then call Natasha Janine later. As I am settling down in my office organizing case files when Natasha Janine walks in.

"Damn Virgie, I have been trying to reach you!"

"Yeah, I got your messages. I was going to call you after I call my clients. You know they are the real people who pay me."

"Girl, fuck that! Do you know what this bitch did?"

Before she could finish, "Is she mad that I went off on her and her hoe in the elevator yesterday?"

"You did what?" I checked they ass. They better find someone to play with because I'm not the one.

"We saw her in my building yesterday. I went off on her for talking to me like we are friends."

Natasha Janine closes my door, "This bitch is trying to blackmail me." What? Hell, no! I should have followed my first mind and popped her in her damn mouth on "GP" like Dominica says, "general purpose."

"She is doing what? I knew I should have kicked her ass in the elevator. How much money does she want? She did the same thing to Dr. Tapes. I definitely should have kicked her ass."

"Virgie what do you mean by she did it to Dr. Tapes? She was messing around with him too. This bitch probably messed around with the whole community. I'm getting a test done."

"Natasha Janine, get to the point. You are acting like me and digressing."

"Virgie, my fault, girl! She doesn't want money. She wants me to lie about that shooting case that happened in your building or she will report me to the ARDC (Attorney Registration and Disciplinary Commission)."

"She what?" Oh, hell no. What the fuck is wrong with her, threatening Natasha Janine's job? Doesn't she know there are enough unemployed people in the world. She should know that fucking with someone else's job isn't cool. I can't tolerate people like that. They are the scum of the earth.

"Yes, she said I took advantage of her when I represented her and that I am harassing her."

"You got to be lying. Damn, that's fucked up! What are you going to do?"

"I hired a lawyer. Do you remember P. Wilson?" Oh, hell no! That man does not have an ethical bone in his body.

"Girl, yes Poochie Wilson ass. He is an awful attorney. He doesn't play by the rules."

"Exactly, I need someone to play by a whole different set of rules who gets the job done. And the fact that he loves me doesn't hurt my chances of winning."

"Natasha Janine, I pray you know what you are doing because you are risking everything. I should go home right now and kick her ass, stinking bitch!"

After hopping it up with Natasha Janine, I was able to get a ton of things accomplished. I returned calls, wrote and filed motions. I have to say, I made up for the time I was away. I actually "worked for my wages," this can't be happening people will start talking. My desk phone is ringing, and I can't help but to smile, it's Mr. Noble.

"Hello, you have reached Virgie Mae Kelly. How may I help you?"

"Babe, are you ready to come home? You have been there all day."

"I will be home soon, wait a minute what is all this home stuff we are talking about."

"My home is your home and there is not a discussion on this matter. What are you doing?"

"You are not going to believe this but I am..."

"Don't tell me Virgie, I know you are not up there earning your keep."

"Yes, I am! I need someone to take me away from here."

"Babe, I can come and get you." He knows I love for him to drive me. I have been driving my whole life so whenever there is an opportunity to ride. I am game.

"I need a couple more hours than I should be ready."

"Hearing your voice made this muscle rock hard, can you help me release?" His muscle moves to my bravado because it understands me. I'm too crazy.

"Really babe, that muscle has no home training. But if I can help, then I will help."

"Close your office door and the blinds!" I jump up from my desk and close that door. I need him like he needs me.

"Ok Mr. Noble, I will fulfill your requests."

"Babe, you were outstanding this morning."

"Well thank you for the compliment, I have to pat myself if I do say so."

"If I was there, I would bend you over and massage that back. I would create that beautiful arch that gives you dimension to your upper and lower stems of your body. Here I am sliding this tight skirt you wore down so I can see those lace pants wrapped around that cushion. Can you feel my hands rubbing over every piece of that material as I'm gripping and massaging your cushion? Can you feel how sensual my touch is? Can you tell how much I miss you? Can you feel the rise of my muscle pushing against your bottom?"

I'm so caught up in this moment that I start answering his questions, "Yes babe I feel your hand, yes I can feel you as I

44

grind against your pants." I love these phone conversations with Noble. He is so descriptive. He always creates a vivid picture of what we are doing. I can tell he really misses me. It's because I fucked his face so hard, he should be recuperating.

He continues to say, "Babe bend over a little. So, I can imagine me perfectly sticking my instruments in the opening of that exit pushing in and out. Out and in then coupling my fingers so you get the power of two. Pushing in and out and out together. Babe, please make that sound I like, so I know you are pleased."

"Oh, oh, and oh!" I'm reminded of this feeling because I love for him to finger me in my ass. You haven't reached a climax until you have experienced the push and pull of two fingers tapping on the inside of your anus.

Noble says, "I love the sound of your "oh," it's so delightful to my ears. I grab hold of your waist squeezing so gently. As I look to see your excitement too, I discover your bodily juices leaking out of those lace panties. So, while you remain bent over, I'm kneeling down on my knees to make sure your area is cleaned up from all spills with the use of my tongue. Because we are in your office and we're not supposed to be doing this in here. I slide your panties over to the side so I can finish licking everything."

"Noble stop this, it is beginning to be too much. I'm sitting here ready to be fucked dripping now from excitement."

"Babe, then touch yourself and tell me what you are doing. I need this, you do too."

"But I'm at work!" I always play the shy girl role. Sometimes it is a role other times I'm really shy. This time I'm playing though.

"This makes it all the better, tell me babe or should I guide you through it." And without even thinking about it I say, "Guide me through it all."

45

"Babe, I put a small item in your bag." I grab my bag and find a small vibrator with a note that says, "use me for your pleasure at work when you think of me!"

"Noble, you gave me a vibrator." What the fuck? I'm too embarrassed to tell him I never had one before. Natasha Janine used to say all the time that I am a virgin to the mic. The mic such as fellatio and toys. She even mentioned a banana once. I still don't know about all that. She tried everything with her nasty ass.

"Yeah babe, it's the size of my hand and smaller than my muscle. I want you to always be pleased but I don't want to be replaced. It is cleaned and sanitized, so you don't have to worry. Now I need you to spread those stems wide and insert in the opening of your choice. I want you to tell me while you do it."

"Well, since we have been discussing my exit, I will insert it in that opening. I'm spreading my stems oh so wide and placing them on my desk. I'm turning on the instrument to feel the vibration in my hand first. I feel the pulsating of it between my fingertips and oh does it feel good. I'm going to have to insert this in me like an enema."

"Babe, keep it sexy and sensual, you just changed the whole mood. Talking about an enema! Babe, you good?" It's over before it started. I'm cracking myself up. I'm too goofy for that.

"I'm sorry I will do better next time, I promise."

"I hope so next time, don't stay there too late. Call me when you are ready, love you lady."

"I sure will." I can definitely mess up a wet dream, too funny. Let me get back to work. I'm still in this office when my office phone rings, "Hello, this is Virgie Mae Kelly! How may I help you?"

"Hello Virgie, this is attorney Sarah McDonald. How are you?"

"I'm good counsel, how may I help you?"

"Virgie, I was wondering if I could speak to you regarding Dr. Winston. I have attempted to contact him for several years regarding a pressing matter and been unsuccessful. It wasn't until Saturday when I saw you both that I am able to acknowledge his whereabouts."

"Counsel, I would suggest you speak directly to him or his attorney regarding any matters. I am currently in a dating relationship with him. I don't think I should be speaking on any legal matters concerning him, his finances, or his past relationships."

"I understand exactly. I just wanted to warn you regarding his past behaviors." Now, I'm curious to know what she is talking about, so I continue on with this discussion. "Sarah can you explain what you mean by that?"

"Virgie, I represented Laverne Lonzetta and her family for many years. Laverne and Noble were high school sweethearts and soulmates until she left this world. She loved him tremendously and he loved her even more. After her death, he became a total wreck. He was reckless with despair. His behavior was an example of a man lost without his soulmate. They had true soul ties. He knew she was ill but didn't do anything to aid her in her healing. Dr. Winston seemed to disconnect from her and the love they shared. It was believed that he was unfaithful and from my understanding it was Laverne's belief too."

"Sarah, how does this have anything to do with me?" Here I am having another conversation about being warned of Noble. She is telling me to guard my heart. I'm so sick of people trying to tell me what's best for me.

"Virgie, it doesn't have anything to do with you. I just want to caution you that Dr. Winston is not who you may think he is." See, this is an example that I should not have even entertained her with this conversation so let me check her right fast.

"Sarah, you haven't seen neither nor spoken to Noble in years. But you felt the need to call me and warn me of a man who loss the love of his life. A man who spent his puberty and his adulthood with this woman. Sarah, I have never loss anyone whom I love the way Noble may have loved Laverne. But if I had I'm sure I wouldn't handle such a devastating tragedy in a professional manner. Instead of warning me of Noble, you should continue to follow through with your clients wishes. You need to sit down with Noble to aid him in the closure he needs for that relationship."

"Virgie, we believe Laverne took her own life. Noble is the only person who knows what really happened. He told us that the autopsy said septic shock as a result from an allergic reaction."

"Sarah, how do you know that's not true?"

"Noble is the only person that saw the medical records. He had them sealed. Since he is the beneficiary of her estate. The night of her death, Laverne called her sister to inform her that she wasn't feeling good and that she was waiting for Noble to come home. She was reaching out to him to come and save her from herself and he did not show up."

"Sarah, I'm so sorry for your loss. It is my prayer that Noble gives you the information and assistance you all need for your closure. But again, this doesn't have anything to do with me. I wish you luck. I need to get back to work, thank you for calling," and I end the call and start thinking.

This man has covered up the death of his first love. Why? What is it that he is afraid would be revealed from her death? Why hasn't he told me the truth? Is there more to the story? Is this why his therapist says he isn't ready to love again? Did he kill her? Why did she do it? Does her family hate him? Is that why he can't sit and listen to her last letter written?

Tuesday

This man has so many hidden compartments to him. Is this why he left the medical field? Is this why he is so protective? So mysterious? There has to be more to this story. Why Noble? Why are you complicated? Why are you so sensual? So irresistible? So charming? Were you a cheater? Are you a cheater? Did you cheat on Laverne? Why are you hiding so many things about your life?

Why are you really seeing a therapist? Who is this therapist? I can spend all my days or all of this week thinking about what is going on with Noble. Noble, why can't we just love each other?

I know I'm not without faults, mistakes and some questionable behavior. So, I am not passing judgement on him. I videotaped myself having sex with Kelle. I even allowed it to be played at a swinger's party. I had no real reason for doing it. I told myself that I was so angry with Kelle as if this was my justification. I did it without his permission. So, I can empathize with people that made mistakes in their past.

I have to call it a wrap, I can't work any longer. I'm sitting here waiting on Noble to pick me up. He isn't normally late, but he did say he would be. Even though I was put on notice, it still feels unusual to have him late. I promise myself that I would not have this discussion about what Sarah shared. I'm wiped out and right now I could use a hug, hot meal, hot shower, and some of that nasty freaky sex he is known for.

I know if I share what I know with Noble, he will want to cut off her head. He is so private. He definitely wouldn't like her sharing his business and what she said about his Laverne. If he did agree with her decision about whether she would live or die, he would support it. Noble is that type of guy. It would be devastating for him to learn that someone wants to leave him here alone. Noble knows that he is a keeper, great lover, domestic male, and a loving provider. But he will remind you from time to time so you can't forget it.

Noble picks me up from the job and is smiling from cheek to cheek. "What are you smiling so hard for?"

"We have to go shopping." Noble knows I hate shopping with him. He has to try on everything and inspect the seams and the zippers.

"I'm too tired for that."

"Ms. Lady knock it off. We have to go shopping for food for our dinner date tomorrow." I am looking at Noble as to say, "What dinner date?"

He immediately responds to my nonverbal communication, "Babe, Jon and MJ are coming over. Have you forgotten about it?"

"Noble, Yes, I did!" Now let me start smiling, my sister is coming over for a date. I wonder if she shared this at her testimony service. It's MJ, she hasn't said a word.

"Babe, we need to get dishes, place setting, and food. I have the housekeeper coming tomorrow morning."

A housekeeper really, "What housekeeper?"

"You don't know everything there is to know about me." He is talking to an empty room because there is no one in here to refute that.

Before I knew it, I say, "there is no lie in that statement."

"Virgie, is that shade you over there throwing?" I'm not throwing shade I'm pointing out the obvious, "Nope, just stating facts Mr. Noble!" Joking with facts or not joking at all.

"Wow, I didn't know I was picking up Ms. Petty Lady. You mad, huh, you are feeling hurt that you don't know everything, wow!" Whatever Noble, whatever!

I say to myself, "That is petty, if I'm leaving it alone then I should leave it alone. Get out of your feelings girl and leave it alone."

We are now home. I am totally exhausted. We went grocery shopping, shopping for place settings, even brought them both gifts for coming to Noble's house. I should say, "our house" since I'm here more than I'm at my own place. Noble is like a little kid around here. "Noble, why are you so happy? You're acting like we are preparing for an engagement party."

"Babe, we are, preparing for an engagement party." He isn't serious, what is he talking about? They have never even had a conversation so how did they get engaged.

"Babe, I'm a believer in energy and mood settings. I want to set the mood. I think they would make a perfect couple and Jon has had his share of failed relationships in the past. I'm rooting for him."

"What do you mean failed relationships?" Jon has a hard time finding love. I don't believe it. He is fine as hell. I would think he is around town breaking hearts left and right.

"Babe, I never told you but the night I met you I was at the concert with Jon." I didn't see him because I would definitely remember him. To be honest, Jon is more my type then Noble.

"I never saw Jon or anyone there with you. I would have definitely remembered."

"Babe, he left and even though I rode with him I stayed. I wasn't ready to go. He originally bought the tickets for him and this lady he was dating at the time, but they broke up before the concert, so I went with him. This is why I believe something is about to happen for him because it was the same thing that happened to me. I found the woman of my life when I wasn't looking for her. It always happens when it is not planned, and this was definitely not planned."

"Noble, if I know anything, I know that my Auntie would fake a heart attack to help MJ to get some."

"What? Are you serious? You think she was faking? No!"

"Noble, you don't know but you will if we keep dating."

"What do you mean "if"? You are stuck with me forever!" I'm rolling my eyes and next thing I know he scoops me up and off to the bedroom we go. This man, this man!

WEDNESDAY

It is early in the AM and my damn thighs are killing me. I think they have been stretched out so far that they may even be bruised. Noble needs to be rewarded for that performance. I wonder, "Does it get better with time or has he reached his peak?"

Every time we are together, I feel like it gets better but what do I know I have only had five different lovers in my lifetime. I'm a relationship kind of girl not someone who randomly gets down. The only thing I did that may be out of character was attend those two swingers' events with my friend Mikki. She was really a bad influence. Mikki is the one who talked me into recording myself with Kelle without his permission and playing the video at her home. Kelle would definitely kill me if he knew.

Those ladies acted like they had never seen a big black dick before. They probably haven't either. Those white women were flocking to the restaurant to see him all the time. They are the reason his business never went under. And he thought it was the pancakes that they were there for. Kelle doesn't have a clue that it was that dick that was bringing in that business.

Mikki, stupid ass bitch, told her friends who he was because in the video you couldn't see our faces just our bodies. This is the main reason why I don't fuck with her ass anymore. Natasha Janine wanted to kill her when I told her what happened. I should have let her do it too. Mikki and Natasha Janine never got a long. Natasha Janine felt like she was only using black men for sex. I haven't seen her ass in about 2 years and knowing her, she is still in that lifestyle.

"Good morning babe! You wore me out last night." That was my only intention. He wears me out too often. For me to return this favor to him makes me really proud.

53

"I wore you out Noble, yeah right, I don't even know if I will be able to walk today." I really wore my damn self out. I'm too sore and can't move.

"Sorry babe, I felt like you needed that. You were so uptight yesterday. I don't know what happened at the office, but you seemed bothered. I thought maybe it had something to do with me because it usually does."

"Yes Noble, I had a lot on my mind. You are right I needed that release. But right now, I am going to get going. I'll take an Uber, so you don't have to get up."

"Babe, I can take you. After all that we did last night, I can't take the chance of some driver sniffing you and discovering you are in heat." We both start laughing, "Noble, you are crazy!"

"I am crazily telling the truth! When a woman is getting love, attention, affection, and sexed down. She can be sniffed down by a hound dog a mile away." Wow, I have never heard any such thing.

While I'm in the bathroom applying my makeup, I hear Noble calling my name. I answer, "Yes Noble?" He says, "Babe, don't wear the red lipstick." What is he talking about?

"Babe, those red lips drive men wild. They make me want to stay locked in this house loving you all day and night. I have a lot of things to do. Do me a favor and wear the nude lips? I need to stay focused."

I walk out the bathroom with a fitted navy-blue suit, my pink pussy blouse, my favorite burgundy loafers, and with my red lipstick on.

"Really babe, you just have to show me who is boss. Wow, I see Ms. Lady doesn't play fair." I roll my eyes and walk to the kitchen to grab a bite to eat before work. I had no intention of wearing red lipstick, so he is right. I just had to show him he is not the boss of me.

We are really enjoying each other's company on the ride to the office. As we proceed westbound on Randolph, I observed my sister Dominica standing in front of my office building. I look over at Noble and he notices it too.

"Why is Dominica waiting on me at my office?" I'm going to regret asking her this. I already know it. If she has come to my office, it's terrible. No one even knew she'd be coming here because they would have warned me.

"That's a great question." He then stops his truck right in front of her. Before I can get out of the truck, Dominica is walking up to the passenger side of the truck.

"Damn, I have been waiting out here for almost an hour. You all be fucking way too much, yawl bogus as shit."

"Girl shut the hell up! What are you doing out here in the first place?"

"Hello Dominica, how are you?" She is standing up smiling up in Noble's face.

"You know me brother-in-law, I'm fair for a square," says Dominica.

"Dominica, what's wrong? You are out here waiting for me and it's 9:21."

"Sister, I need to talk to you! It's important, very important!"

"Is there anything I can do to help you Dominica?" What the hell is going on here? She is playing with me. And she is here on some psychotic episode shit.

"No, I'm good! I just need to holler at my sister." There is a lie in this but where I may never know.

I then hurry up and get out of the truck to hear what's going on. Dominica never asks for help until it's the last minute, so I need to really find out what's going on. Noble also hurried out of the truck to assist me and by the time he makes it to my door, I stepped out and is standing on the curve. He leans in to give me a hug and says, "Babe, let me open the door when you are riding with me. Those couple of seconds in time will not make a difference but you're rushing out of this truck, can. Be careful, love you," then kisses me.

He says to Dominica, "I hope everything is good but if not please let me know what I can do to help."

"Thanks man, I appreciate it," then reaches out to hug him. I look at her like "what the hell" because something is definitely wrong, she hates PDA (public displays of affection).

"Okay enough of that, let's go so I can figure out how to help you."

Noble laughs because he thinks I'm jealous but I'm not or maybe I am but so what. I roll my eyes at him as Dominica, and I are walking into the building.

We are walking into the building and as soon as we clear the door, I turn to her and say, "What the fuck is going on?"

"Virgie, I'm pregnant! I don't know what to do." What the hell? Oh, hell no! Pregnant? She couldn't be serious, pregnant!

"You're pregnant? By whom? You are what? Pregnant? Are you serious?"

"I'm pregnant by Fatel and he keeps fighting me. I'm tired of him hitting me and I just don't know what to do."

I drop my bags and reach out to hug her. I'm at a loss for words. She is still a baby, a grown baby, but still a baby.

"First, you are going to be alright. Don't worry about taking care of this child. Secondly, I'm going to kill that motherfucker for putting his hands on you. Mark my words, "I'm going to kill him!"

"Virgie, that's why I'm here. I told Twaab and her and some of her gay friends jumped on him and beat him very badly."

"Twaab, you told her before you told me? Wow, she hasn't said a word!"

"Sister, can you let this conversation be about me for a minute. I need your help!"

"I'm sorry! I digress! When we get to my office, please tell me what you need for me to do."

We're on the elevator and I start thinking to myself. Dominica is not ready for no child and Fatel damn sure isn't ready. I'm still fucking him up when I see him, bitch ass chump. He is a lazy mother fucker. He needs his ass kicked on a daily basis. I knew something wasn't right about him when I met him.

Fatel has really fucked up now. He has the nerve to put his hands on my sister after she took care of his chump ass when he got shot in his ass and couldn't sit down for a month. I will definitely be kicking him in that ass when I see him. He better not say nothing. I can't wait until we get off this elevator and in my office. I'm burning up inside with anger! I need more details about this.

My thoughts are interrupted when Dominica says, "Sister, you really be talking to yourself. When we were younger, I used to say that's why Virgie is so smart because she processes everything with her imaginary friend before she does anything."

I bust out laughing, "Dominica shut the hell up," then I think about it like "she ain't wrong" and I continue to laugh.

We are at the reception area and I tell my secretary Tabitha to hold all my calls. Before I can close the door good, I see Noble calling my phone and I answer it.

"Babe, is everything okay with your sister?" He knows I have some information. I wasn't going to wait until we were in the office to get it, but I can't share it with him at this time.

"Noble, we just walked into the office. I will call you back." I end the call and I notice Dominica is crying. "Sister, what is wrong?"

"I'm pregnant and Fatel is not the daddy!" This is the stuff that drives me crazy. She just told me he is the daddy now he isn't.

"What? Then who is the daddy?" She better know. This damn lady.

"I don't know, I can't remember shit!" See, why Lord? Why? She can't remember nothing.

"Are you fucking kidding me? You can't fucking remember who you are having sex with? I'm signing you into the hospital. You have lost your damn mind forever. Is this why Fatel is fighting you?"

"No sister, Fatel is constantly fighting me. I just never said anything. I'm tired of it."

"So, Dominica, what do you need my help with?" I bet she doesn't even know.

"I am not ready to have a baby, but I don't want an abortion either. I want you to have this baby." What? Oh hell, no! I'm not ready for a baby. I just found a man who loves me. I'm being punked.

"Are you fucking serious? You couldn't be fucking serious? Stop fucking playing! Are you fucking serious? Dominica, what the fuck?"

"Sister, you are the only stable person who can do it." Now there is some truth and lie in this statement. Nevertheless, I'm not ready for a baby and definitely not ready to deal with her and Fatel's shit either.

"Have you told MJ about this?" MJ will have to take this child. She is the person who decided to be the guardian for her ass.

"No, I haven't told anyone." Oh, really Dominica. You just drop this shit off into my lap, really.

"What do you mean you haven't told anyone? Then why is Fatel so mad?" See, here we go again. Damn, we should have forced her to get her mind right.

Wednesday

"Virgie, we were at my place and I wasn't feeling good. I was talking to Twaab on the phone and telling her I wasn't feeling good. Fatel came into the room and demanded I give him my phone, so we start arguing. Twaab said her and some of her friends were about to dip out and that she would stop over and bring me something to eat."

"You don't have any food in your house?" Why the fuck is she at that damn apartment without food? She never has to do without. I should pop her ass back to reality. She makes me sick.

"No, I don't! Fatel got mad at me. He said I'm fronting on him because I'm acting like he can't feed me, and he was letting me starve."

"First of all, that's not his fucking house, bitch ass chump!" She is letting him act like he is the king of that castle. Bum ass clown, good for nothing fool, goofy ass man with his scary ass. I'm going to kick his ass.

"Virg, let me finish! Fatel started complaining about how I have fucked up his life. He hates me. So, I told him "bye" then he hauled off and slapped me."

"That bitch slapped you in your face? I am going to kill him. He doesn't put his damn hands on you!"

"Yeah, that's it he slapped me! Because I'm pregnant, I wasn't trying to fight with him. Twaab used her key and came into the apartment. She must've heard us. She opened the door, grabbed him by his head, and started punching him in the face. For a minute, I just watched her beat his ass. He broke away and said he was getting his gun. I didn't even know he had a gun. Twaab, ran out the front door but she came back with this girl or guy. I can't really remember but they snatched that rusty ass gun from Fatel and whooped his ass. He had knots on his head and ass. He was bleeding from his mouth as well as his head.

Twaab 'nem left and I was stuck in the house with his ass, so I called for paramedics. They wanted to arrest me for beating his ass. I told them I was pregnant and was experiencing morning sickness. Shit, I was not going to jail for that, fuck him. He was the one who ran and got a gun with his stupid ass."

"Where is Twaab?"

"I don't know!"

"So, what do you need my help for."

"I told you I want you to take care of this baby because I'm about to go to jail and I ain't ready to be a mother."

"Dominica, you are not going to jail!"

"Well tell that to the police. They came to the apartment this morning and said I have 24 hours to tell them who did it because Fatel is not going to make it. So, I came straight here!"

"Are you fucking serious? So Twaab tried to kill him before I did. Damn, that's fucked up!"

"Sister, you crazy as hell! I'm about to go to jail. You are here talking about Twaab did it before you. Now, that's fucked up."

I chuckled, "You're right let me call Twaab, to get over here. Does she know you are pregnant?"

"Damn Virg, yawl be tripping about how I forget shit. You're the one who be forgetting shit and talking to imaginary friends. I told you that you are the only person I told, damn!"

I can't stand her crazy ass, but she is right. I call Twaab on the speakerphone, "Sister, I have Dominica here, so we need you to come down here."

"I was already on my way down there. I saw Noble at the grocery store. He told me that Dominica was at your job and she looked terrible."

Dominica says, "Fuck Noble, his ass smells good!"

Me and Twaab both are laughing hysterically while she is sitting here rolling her eyes at us.

Shortly after, Twaab and Zam are walking into my office looking stressed. "Sister, why did you bring Zam?"

"Because Zam is the one who kicked Fatel's ass. I'm not strong enough to fight. I just got out of the hospital!" I forgot that I have to decipher through Dominica's conversation. There are tons of details she has all mixed up. Not to mention, Twaab just got out of the hospital from the car accident. She walks with a cane. Her leg is in a cask. Zam says, "Hey Ms. Virgie."

Zam is Twaab's best friend who is a transgender male. He and Twaab roll together no matter what, like Natasha Janine and me.

They have been friends forever. He is the big guy Dominica was talking about because as a woman he would be described as being tall. As a man, he is 250lbs, 6'2" and strong. He is quick tempered but overall a nice guy.

"Twaab, what happened sister?" I need to speak with someone who has some sense. Dominica is driving me crazy. I may check myself into the hospital to get my mind back right after this conversation.

Dominica says, "Virgie, I just told you!" Shut the hell up! You haven't told me a damn thing.

"Okay now let Twaab and Zam tell what they saw. I will get you all some chairs," I then walk out and retrieve two chairs.

When I return back into the office, everyone is laughing so I say, "What's so funny?"

Twaab says between laughs, "Dominica says she is pregnant and you and Noble are adopting the baby, she is crazy! She isn't pregnant."

"How do you know? If she believes she is, then she very well may actually be pregnant."

"I'm not pregnant. I just said that to see how you bitches would react. Well, I might be because I haven't had a period in about two months or maybe three."

61

"I know this, you will definitely be taking a pregnancy test as soon as they tell me what happened."

Twaab immediately starts talking, "Dominica called me and was talking about she was hungry. I told her that Zam was taking me to therapy. I would bring her some money to get something to eat. When we get there, I hear her and Fatel arguing which isn't anything unusual. This bum ass dude was talking about he would kill her.

So, I entered the apartment first and walked up on him. He had his hand raised like he was going to hit her, and I grabbed his arm. That chump turns like he was going to hit me. Before I knew it Zam knocked his ass all the way across the room. He jumped up and wanted to fight. Zam whooped his ass. We then left Dominica with the money and bounced."

Dominica says, "Yeah I called the police on his ass because he stole my money and left.

When I called him about it, he hung up on me and said, "fuck you" with his stupid ass."

"Dominica, you told me that Twaab and her friends beat him bloody, and you called the paramedics."

"Damn sister, it's all the same thing!"

All you can hear is us yelling in unison, "No it isn't!" Dominica has the nerve to start laughing at us. This woman is going to give me a heart attack.

Dominica then says, "That's why they probably gave me this paper right here" pulling a police report from her pocket. I snatched the report, "This is a RD report for theft does not assault and battery."

"I know that's why I brought it to you so I can see what else I need to do."

"Twaab, take her ass to the store and get her a pregnancy test. This damn girl is trying to send me to an early grave. Dominica, your ass told me a whole different story."

Wednesday

Let me tell you, this morning has been absolutely crazy. I called Noble and told him everything and he laughed his ass off. I don't think Dominica shit is funny, let me stop lying some of it is quite funny. I hope and pray she is not pregnant. This is definitely not what I would need, taking custody of a baby. Then dealing with Dominica and whoever supposed to be that child's father.

Now, I need to prepare my mind for this dinner date with MJ and Jon. My sister is probably going to be nervous I should call her to see if she is okay. Let me dial her from my desk so at least I could finish up this paperwork while I talk to her.

"Hello," says MJ.

"Hey sister, you would not believe what happened today!" I have to tell her about this crazy girl.

"Virgie, I already know," what was I thinking? I knew Twaab was going to tell her.

"How do you know? Did Twaab call you?" Watch she says Twaab called her. Twaab is always trying to tell something before I do.

"No, Dominica called me! She called to tell me she is pregnant, and you made her take a test. She says it's your fault because she wouldn't have known she was pregnant if you had minded your own business." This damn lady is truly deranged.

"What the hell is she talking about? She came to my office and told me her business."

"Virgie, we are going to have to figure this out. Twaab confirmed that she is indeed pregnant." Pregnant! Oh my God! Pregnant, meaning with child. What?

"You got to be fucking kidding me. Are you fucking serious?"

"I'm not kidding but we can talk about this tomorrow because tonight I have a date!" Damn, what was I thinking. My man and I are hosting this dinner.

"Sister, you better say that!" That's my sister, come get your man.

"Virgie, I have a question. Do I need to shave down there?" What the what? She is really trying to claim her man. She isn't wrong.

"MJ, you are trying to get you some, damn, you a freak," as I laugh hysterically.

"Virgie, I just have not paid any attention to that area before, but I want to feel like my best self just in case we hit it off."

"Definitely, but all I suggest is that you be you, fabulous and all. Do you want me to come and get you or are you taking an Uber?"

"I'll get there, just prepare for my arrival." Prepare is what we will do. We definitely need to set the mood. Noble was right but I'm not telling him.

"Well, you better arrive then. See you in a few. Love you sister."

I end the call and the first thing comes to my mind is "Dominica is pregnant," damn!

I order an Uber to pick me up so Noble can finish whatever he is doing. My cell phone is ringing, and I see it's Noble's friend Raq calling me, so I answer.

"What's up Raq?"

"Hey Virgie, I'm trying to reach Noble it's kind of important."

"Raq, he should be at the condo because we are about to have dinner with Jon and my sister in about an hour."

"Okay, I have called him a couple of times and he hasn't answered."

"Well, I should be there shortly and will let Noble know as soon as I arrive."

"Thanks Virgie, let him know it's important."

"Will do, take care Raq!" Why would he call me? Maybe Noble told him about him falling out last week and he is worried. What does he want and why isn't Noble answering his call?

I'm going to call. I pray my baby hasn't had another episode. I know he has been running around all day making sure everything is perfect.

"Hey babe, Raq called me. He said he had been trying to reach you and you're not answering. What's going on? Are you okay?"

"Babe, I know what Raq wants, and he will have to wait. I'm in a good space and he wants to bombard me with his foolishness."

"Oh okay, I'm pulling up now. Babe, do you think we have time for me to be pleased after my shower. I need to release this day has been a tornado of emotions."

"Babe, you don't ever have to ask me that. I have prepared you a hot bath. I am anticipating your arrival. Remember it's my Uber account that you are using. I have been tracking your ride in case this driver smells that heat I talked about earlier."

I'm smiling from cheek to cheek and when I look up, I can see the driver smiling cheek to cheek too. He heard me ask for some from my man. I bet he is sitting up there at full attention with his nosey ass.

I get out of the Uber walking towards the door. I feel my cell phone vibrating and I see it's my sister MJ calling.

"Sister, what's wrong?" I just talked to her. Why is she calling me back? She better not have changed her mind about this dinner date.

"Virgie, what the hell is going on?" MJ is cursing, this has to be really serious if she is cursing.

"Sister, what are you talking about and why are you cursing," and I start listening intently to what she has to say.

"Virgie, Dominica called me saying that the police are looking for Fatel because he assaulted you about this baby."

MJ knows we have to decipher what Dominica is saying, and she knows we never can take what she says at face value because there is always more to the story.

"Sister, you should be trying to prepare for a great time tonight, don't worry about Dominica, and let's figure out what our little sister is talking about tomorrow."

"Virgie, but should I be worried about her?" I want to say "yes." But I instead say, "Sister please let me prepare for your arrival, you have a date tonight. I love you sister and I will see you soon," and I end the call.

I use my key to enter the apartment and when I opened the door, I noticed that Jon already arrived for dinner. "Noble I'm home!" While giving him the side eye glare looking at Jon sitting on the couch, I was supposed to be pleased before the party. Why is he here so early?

Noble sees the look I'm giving to him and says, "Babe, Jon arrived early because he may have to leave if the ER is swamped with patients..." Jon interjects saying, "I really need this distraction so I pray all is well in the city and the ER can handle it without me."

"Hello Jon, it is good to see you again!"

"I'm so sorry Virgie it is quite rude of me not to speak, hello young lady. I hope your sister has not stood me up. I'm excited to get to know her." Now I like that. My sister is all that and more, so he better not be disappointing. MJ has turned down tons of dates and to get her to agree with this date is a feat of its own.

Noble interrupts my thoughts when he comes to take my bags and gives me one of those provocative wet kisses, he loves to share.

He then leads me into the bedroom and closes the door. "Mr. Noble, we have a guest."

Wednesday

"First off, I didn't tell him to come over this early he decided that on his own. Nevertheless, I explained to him that I had not seen you all day, and when you arrive that I would be committing some time to you. So, I told him that you may need to unwind before we can begin our dinner."

"Noble, but I asked to be pleased, I have had a long day and all I want and excuse my French is to be "fucked from behind!" I know he hates that word but that's how I feel, and I just had to say it.

"Babe, I'm here, "as you would have me," so why do you feel like I wouldn't do that for you?"

"Ah, duh, Jon is sitting in the living room!"

And before I could finish what I am saying, Noble is bending me over and is removing my panties with his hand. He takes his fingers, and he is rubbing my ass and squeezing my pussy. I'm in shock of how fast this has happened that I can't even remember the words he has given these body parts. It feels wonderful. His hand is so warm like he had it in hot water before I walked in the house. There it is! Oh, right there he has stuck his finger right inside "oh yeah my sweet muscle."

"Noble, this feels so good. Thank you, baby, thank you I needed this. Baby, this is so intense, oh baby, how many fingers do you have in there? Oh baby, oh, oh, oh baby…"

Noble starts talking over me and says, "I'm fucking you with three fingers, can you feel them? Because when I stick my dick in here, we need to make it quick because we have a guest." I am dead standing! Is this man saying, "fucking and dick?" I can't believe he just said what I think he just said. Next thing I know, he is doing just as he said and now, he is fucking me in the middle of the room. I'm losing my balance, but I grab hold of my legs and pushing back against him with all of my might. And he is relentless and wearing my ass out. I have to be careful of what I ask for because he is undoubtedly "fucking" me.

"Babe, I need you to squeeze this pussy tighter so I can cum!"

"Oh okay, okay," I do as I'm told, and he erupts like a volcano. It's dripping on the floor. I stand up and turn to kiss him and say, "Noble, you are definitely right! Those words take the passion out of it and it's the passion that makes it happen for me." He lifts me up and kisses me back and says, "whatever you need I am willing to give, I love you babe!"

I cleaned up behind our quick sexual encounter and then I took a bath. I see while we were getting it on that I missed a call from Natasha Janine. I call her back, but she doesn't answer. I wonder has that bitch said or did anything else since we last talked. I call my sister Twaab to tell her about how Jon is excited. He came over early because he is frantic to meet a Kelly girl.

"Hey Twaab, what are you doing?" I'm bored and don't want to sit in their faces while they talk.

"Virgie Mae, I told you about asking questions you don't want to know the answers to." She makes me sick with her smart mouth-ass, but I love her still.

"Did MJ tell you she has a date with Dr. Tapes at Noble's place?"

"Sister, you know she did! She is so nervous. I just helped her get dressed because I'm staying with her."

"Why are you staying there? What is wrong with your place?" They kill me with this I'm the last person to know what's going on. But as soon as they need something, I'm the first person they call.

"Virgie, I have been having nightmares after the crash, so MJ told me to stay with her.

I'm good so don't worry. My PCP is referring me to a therapist to deal with this."

"Sister, I'm sorry to hear this but you are doing the best thing staying with MJ. She is around there treating you like a baby. Has MJ left yet?"

"No, she hasn't, she is waiting for her ride now. She is super nervous so don't be having her in the hot seat for too long. She will keep me up all night. What am I talking about she is going to keep me up anyway?"

"Well sister, if you want, you can spend some nights at my place. I can come home, and we can kick it there too."

"Thanks sister, I'm good. Be with your man! I think I may stay with Dominica to keep an eye on her and since she is pregnant somebody will need to."

"We are going to need to have a family meeting to figure this thing out and definitely to get a handle on it."

"Virgie, I called and made her appointment to see the doctor so the nurse will be calling back tomorrow with that date. We all can go with her and discuss it then." She is right. We can figure it out when we have more information.

I walk into the living room. I see Noble is in a happy place. I can tell he really kicks it with Jon. They are talking, laughing and watching sports. Noble turns and sees me standing in the kitchen and say, "Babe, you need me to get you something? Jon, excuse me let me check on my babe."

He walks up to me and kisses me and says, "I missed you when you were bathing!" I smile and shake my head saying to myself, this man, this man!

We are all talking when the front desk calls. It's Anthony, the doorman, he is informing us that Marion is here. I can't wait to tell my Auntie that MJ used her government name. She is going to go off. This family of mine. They keep you laughing, crying, confused, and entertained, Marion is here!

I tell Noble let me go meet her at the elevator in case she needs to be touched up or something. I walk to the elevator in the hall and when the door opens, I damn near passed out. My sister MJ looks drop dead gorgeous. She didn't hold back on any punches. She has thick hair that she always wears in a bun but not today. Her hair is straightened with big, beautiful curls. She has on an emerald-colored belle bottom pantsuit, a turquoise blouse with a peek of her breast being exposed, big gold hoop earrings, some Gucci heels, her Burberry coat draped across her arm, and a bright red lipstick.

"Damn, sister! You came to claim your man!"

"Virgie, do I look good? Twaab picked this outfit out from my closet," as she rubbed alongside of her suit. "How do I look?"

"Sister, you look beautiful! I need her to style me, damn!" Twaab did that for her BFF. I give MJ a big hug as we walk into the condo. I stop at the door and I say, "Gentleman, please can I have your attention, I present to you all Ms. Marion Kelly!"

MJ says, "I hope I haven't had you all waiting long for me." Noble is standing up with his mouth open. Jon immediately walks to the door and takes her coat and says, "Ma'am, it was worth the wait!" He better go on and flatter my sister, she deserves it because she did that.

I walk over to Noble and say, "Close your mouth because you have a lady," as I grab his hand and starts chuckling. He hugs me and says, "Lucky for you, because if I didn't, I would have to knock Jon over the head for your sister." He plays way too much. But the truth is if she wasn't my sister and I was into girls, I would have pushed up on her myself. She is damn fine! My sister Twaab hooked MJ up, damn!

Noble takes MJ's coat from Jon as Jon escorts her over to the couch. I stay in the dining area with Noble so that they can talk. Noble and I watch the two of them laughing. We see Jon touch her hand a couple of times. MJ looks so happy and carefree. Jon is smiling and laughing as if he is pleased with the conversation that is taking place. Jon asks, "Noble, what time is dinner?"

Noble says, "Whenever you all would like to eat," he then leans to whisper in my ear, "I'm ready to eat myself and grabs my thigh." I smack his hand as a sign to behave but he doesn't. Noble then says, "You all please excuse us for a minute. I need to discuss something with Virgie before we eat."

Jon says without even looking at us, "We will be fine, I promise to be the perfect gentleman in your absence."

Noble grabs my hand and leads me into the bedroom. "Noble, we can't, sweetie I don't want us seen as bad hosts. My sisters are going to kill me for leaving MJ alone with Jon." I'm saying as he is kissing my neck, my face, my breast, my lips between words.

"Babe, that was Jon's signal for us to leave the room. We discussed it." I pushed Noble back and say, "He is trying to have sex with my sister on the first date, in my damn living room, while we all are here! Hell no, he…"

Noble interrupts me by grabbing my arm and says, "He is not trying to disrespect your sister. He just wanted to talk to her alone. I told him if he is enjoying her company to ask about the food and we will give them some privacy."

"Noble, when was this information going to be passed along to me?"

"Babe, I'm telling you now."

"How long is this privacy shit supposed to happen?" I'm too mad with him and Jon plotting shit against my sister.

"Babe, we never said. We didn't work out all of the details." Hell, no I'm going in there with my sister. I get up off the bed and walk right in the living room with Jon and MJ.

I say to MJ, "You good sister?" She is sitting up smiling cheek to cheek and says, "I'm great sister, what's wrong?"

Before I can say a word, Noble says, "It's time for dinner!" Jon gets up and extends his hand to get MJ up and I say, "She is good! Help Noble in the kitchen." He goes.

I lean into MJ and asks, "Is he trying to have sex with you?" She gives me the "clinch your pearls" look.

"Virgie Mae, are you serious? We are sitting here talking. Why would you think that?"

"Because sister he and Noble had a code word so he could be alone with you. And if he was fresh with you, I'm sending his ass home." MJ is laughing, and laughing a little too hard if you ask me, "What's funny?"

"Virgie, he told me about it when you all went into the room, but he said that since he and Noble didn't discuss how we would be left alone that he said scratch the idea. Jon was really asking about dinner because we both are hungry. I told him if my sister finds out she will go off and here you are going off," as she continues to laugh.

"MJ, so you are not nervous to be alone with him?" I know my sister is not a wild lady. I don't need another surprise today.

"Virgie, it would have been fine." I reach out and give her a hug. My big sister is growing up on me, I'm so proud.

Dinner was great. We really had a good time. We laughed, played Uno, listened to music, played karaoke, and talked for hours. It was 11:09 p.m. and I was nervous about Jon dropping my sister off at home. I made MJ call me on the ride home and as soon as they pulled up at her door. I made her promised not to sit in the car talking and to get out immediately then go inside. I called Twaab to be looking out the window and watch him the whole time to see if he tries to kiss her. Noble just sat on the couch laughing at me talking about Jon is nothing like Raq and that Jon likes MJ. He is very respectful.

"Yeah, you were very respectful too until you weren't any more if you know what I mean."

72

Wednesday

"Babe, I don't know what you mean. I never said to them how I took you in the room because I was hungry for this sweet muscle. Or how I wanted to taste it before dinner," while rubbing in between my legs. I have learned to delight in this feeling, so I decided to keep them open while he does it.

MJ calls me during this process so Noble tells me to keep talking and I do. He lays me down on the couch and starts wetting my muscle with his tongue. MJ is telling me she made it home and how her and Jon are going to church together on Sunday. She says she gave him her number. He said he will call her when he makes it home.

"Ouch!" MJ asks, "What happen? Are you okay?" I tell her I'm fine, I dare not tell her what Noble is doing to this sweet muscle while I'm talking to her on the phone. He just thrusted himself inside of me and it took me by surprise. MJ thanks us for dinner and says tell Noble thank you. I repeat what she says and Noble says, "Thanks for coming," but I think that comment is really for me

THURSDAY

We had such a great night, double dating, I hope Jon and MJ hit it off so we can do more of that. Noble was definitely in his element being the "host." I was so surprised how down to earth my sister is, Twaab always said that MJ was cool to hang out with, but I never tried it. After last night I will definitely make time on my schedule to hang out with my big sister more often.

I really like Jon too. He was so cool and suave. He is fun, personable, easy on the eyes, and has a great smile. Just like Noble said about my sister I can say it about Jon, "If I didn't have a man, I would probably knock my sister over the head for him." Noble is too funny. I really love how attentive Jon was to MJ. He kept smiling at her like he just hit the lottery jackpot. I peeped how he was mildly flirting with her. You know when a person is "flirting" but not really flirting. He always seemed to find a reason to whisper in her ear. I can't wait to call her when I get into the office and find out what he was saying. MJ was giggling too hard, batting her long eyelashes, and twirling her curls over and over. The world better take notice of her relationship with God because she would be breaking hearts in these streets. I'm sure of it.

"Good morning, Babe! I see you're up, doing your thinking again" he says and starts laughing.

"Whatever Noble! I was just reminiscing on our dinner date yesterday."

"Babe, I thought you were going to say on me pleasing you last night." This man always wants feedback on his performance.

"Noble, you did that! Do you feel better knowing I'm always well pleased?"

Thursday

"Babe, that's what I love to hear because if I need to change it up, you know I'm game. What time do you want me to take you to the office?" Noble thinks he has to drive Ms. Lady to work whenever I stay the night. Today is such a nice day, I am going to walk to get some exercise.

"Noble, I will walk to work. Have you talked to Raq yet? I saw he called your phone last night."

"So, we are in real love when we start checking each other's phone." I wasn't really checking his phone I just glanced over when it flashed.

"For your information Mr. Noble, I don't need to check phones. I know what I want to know and that's enough for me." Take that Noble, you don't know me like that.

"Okay, Ms. Lady! I did see that he called me again last night. I texted him and told him I would get with him after I drop you off at work. Raq believes his issues and problems must supersede everyone else's. People should drop everything to aid him with his shit. Sometimes I have to shut him down before I run to assist him with his matters. I love the dude, but I often wonder when he will grow up and stop this middle-age crisis shit."

"Do you think his issues have anything to do with Mari and Shenine? I didn't tell you that Mari is trying to blackmail Natasha Janine and to think about it she called me yesterday too. I am going to call her now."

"Babe, please don't. When we are in this bed, in this house, together and enjoying each other's company, let this time be about us. They will forever need us, but I need us to always make it about us first." This is really why I love this man. He loves me enough to make what matters to him all about me.

Even though Noble insisted that he takes me to work, I won that fight because I am walking to the office, but he tagged along.

75

We need this exercise or do we really. We are having a great deal of sex so I'm sure that accounts for exercise too. As we walk to my office, heads are turning left and right at us holding hands and Mr. Noble carrying my purse. They are probably looking at him like "he's gay" but if they only knew the truth. Well, I will keep that to myself unless I share it with Natasha Janine. I need to call her as soon as I walk into the office.

We made it to the office in one piece, "Noble, are you walking me upstairs so you can call for a ride to take you back home?" I know he doesn't want to walk back.

"Babe, I will walk back! It's beautiful outside and it's always beautiful downtown." I think he may be ill, he wants to walk back home, wow! "Babe, I will walk to your office then go home." This is really strange because he never wants to come inside of the building.

After walking me into the office I see Noble speaking to my receptionist Tabitha. I bet he is checking with her concerning my schedule. He is up to something and when he leaves, I will definitely find out. I am settling down getting some case files in order when my phone rings.

"Good morning, this is Virgie Mae Kelly! How may I help you?" I'm saying to myself, "why didn't Tabitha answer the phone?"

"Virgie, this is Raq!" Why is he calling my office?

"Hey Raq! How may I help you?" He doesn't want me, he wants Noble.

"Virgie, I am trying to get in touch with Natasha Janine. I have been calling her and I have been unable to reach her. Do you know how I could get in touch with her?"

"Raq, I just walked into the office. I haven't spoken to her but is there something I could help you with?"

"Virgie, can you just contact her and have her to contact me? It's kind of important. My other line is ringing but please reach out to her for me and have her to call me immediately."

"Okay, will do. Take care!" What the fuck is going on? I bet this has something to do with them damn bitches. Let me call her now.

I call Natasha Janine and she doesn't answer. I text her, facetime her, and call her home phone. There is still no answer. I call her office to see if she had to work and her receptionist Naomi answers. "Hey Naomi, is Ms. Fitzgerald in the office."

"Ms. Kelly, she has court this morning but I have not been able to reach her. Her client called the office looking for her because she didn't show up." What the fuck?

Something happened, I need to go to her house if she is at home.

"Well, thank you Naomi for your help. If she does come into the office, please have her call me at her earliest convenience," and I end the call.

I grab my bag and tell Tabitha to hold all my calls. I will be out of the office for a couple of hours. I haven't even checked my schedule to see if I have any appointments, I am out the door hopping into a cab.

The cab drops me off at Natasha Janine's house. We had always made a pack to keep keys to each other's place just in case. We used to party really hard out there in these streets and wanted to make sure we could come to the other person's rescue if needed. I used my keys to enter her house and I can see something is wrong. Natasha Janine has OCD (obsessive compulsive disorder) and this place is a mess. She would die if she came home and saw this place.

"Natasha Janine, are you here? Natasha, where the fuck are you?" If she is in here, I know how to get her to respond. I start screaming, "Na-Na, baby girl! I miss you Na, Na, Na!"

"Virgie, cut that shit out!" She is here. I knew she would respond to that. Ever since our college days, she has hated someone shortening her name. We went on a double date and the guy she was with kept calling her "Na, Na, Na!" She told me then that no one would ever call her anything but by her given names. And she didn't care if people wanted to or not.

Natasha Janine walks out into the living room from the basement in a robe looking a mess. She is disheveled with bags underneath her eyes. She looks like she's been crying too.

"What's wrong with you? Why haven't you answered any of my calls? You didn't show up for court. Are you losing your damn mind?"

"Virgie, I fucked up. This bitch is trying to destroy me!" I knew that bitch Mari had something to do with this.

"What the fuck did she do? Raq called me yesterday looking for Noble and today he called looking for you at my office. What the fuck is really going on here?"

"Virgie, I hate Raq's trifling ass. He is the reason I'm so fucked. This bitch Mari stole Raq's videotape from his house of that ménage à trios shit we did. I didn't even know this mother fucker videoed it. Mari told me that Raq's mother fucking ass videos everything at his place. Shenine stole the video. She has had it the whole time. Can you believe this bitch Raq didn't even know it was gone until I called his punk ass about it? Now he is calling you and Noble about the shit." I can't even believe the words that are coming out of her mouth.

"Natasha Janine, this is fucked up! Are you serious?" Please let her be playing. This is crazy! It is getting crazier by the day.

"Virgie, I am locked in this damn house, walking around in a robe, I left my client abandoned in court, I have not returned one single phone call, and my house looks a mess. Now ask yourself, am I serious?" I'm speechless, this shit keeps getting worse as time goes on.

"Virgie, I told Raq mother fucking ass to report the video stolen but his ass says there is footage on there that cannot be exposed. I told his ass, "Yeah my shit is on there and that shit can't be exposed either," but his ass is talking about that there is some incriminating footage on the video, and he wouldn't give me any further information regarding the matter. Girl, these damn people really are trying to destroy my life."

"Natasha Janine, I don't have any words to say. I am so sorry you are in this position with these scoundrels. Noble told me that this is Mari and Shenine's thing. He said that they work together and run these kinds of scams on people. They are so young and so fucked up! They will not have a chance in this world. What did Poochie Wilson have to say about this?"

"Virgie, he is telling me not to worry. How can I do that when these bitches keep fucking with me?"

"Girl, you can't stay here buried in the basement avoiding people either. You are one of the best criminal defense attorneys I know and that speaks a lot since I know so many. You need to approach this thing, like you would if you were the attorney representing your client and your ultimate outcome is to win at all cost. Those bitches may know the streets, but they don't know law, you know that." I say as I am handing her a paper towel to wipe her face. She is going to have to command her life back from these bitches.

"Is there anything you need to do? I will have Noble talk to Raq ass too. I still can't believe his ass is mixed up in this shit too."

"Virgie, thank so much for coming over. I was lying downstairs because I didn't even want anyone to look in my window and see me. I knew eventually you would find me. You are the only person I trust but when I tell you I want to kill that bitch, I want to kill that bitch…"

I immediately interject and say, "I want to kill her ass too! But, where she and her hoe fucked up at is, we have the law on our side. And we are damn good at using it too. Mark my words, those bitches will get what's coming to them. They fucked with the wrong people! And for whoever is rolling with them, they can get some of this too! Fuck Raq ass too even if he is Noble's friend!"

"You right Virg, I need to pull this shit together and I need to do it now. Can you stay here while I get dressed and we can go back to the office together?"

"Girl, you don't have to ask me that. I will call Noble about this shit and see what information if any he has about this." She thanks me and proceeds to clean up before she gets dressed. That is definitely that OCD shit.

I call Noble and he doesn't answer. I wonder if he is on the phone with Raq's ass. Raq is everything I thought he was. He stays in some shit and hot water. I need to find out how he and Noble became friends in the first place. I see how Jon and Noble are friends, they are similar in a lot of ways. They both are doctors, fine, nice, sexy as hell, respectful and loving. Raq's ass is the total opposite. I thought that he wouldn't involve Natasha Janine in this shit. Simply, because she is my friend and I'm dating his friend. You would think, but this damn man apparently doesn't think.

Why the hell would he video somebody without permission? I need to move on because I have done the same shit. I think I better tell Kelle about the video I took and shared without his permission. Damn, me and Raq are the same type of people. I am not shit either. I hate Mikki ass.

Natasha Janine interrupts my thoughts saying, "Virgie, I'm okay and instead of going into the office I will work from home. I will call my office and clients. I will let them know I'm not feeling well. You can go back to the office I'll be fine and thanks for checking up on me."

"Girl stop acting like we aren't family. I can work from here too. I will have Noble pick me up later. Are you hungry? I can place a delivery order." I start laughing, but she doesn't. She is definitely feeling bad because she loves my corny jokes.

I feel my phone vibrating. I see it is Noble calling and I answer saying in my seductive tone, "Hey my Noble, what are you doing? I called you, you didn't answer. Well, I didn't want to leave a message. What's wrong?" I can't believe the way he is talking to me, talking to Virgie like this.

"I'm at Natasha Janine's house. I'm helping her with something. Have you talked to Raq yet? Well, I will be over here for a couple of hours. Can you pick me up about six? Okay, I will see you soon," I know he didn't just hang up without a "bye babe." I bet Noble's attitude has something to do with Raq's ass. I just bet it does!

Natasha Janine walks back into the room as I am ending my call. "Virgie, was that Noble on the phone? Did he talk some sense into his damn friend? Please tell me I can rest easy?"

"Yes, it was him, but he was going off about me leaving work and not telling him. He said he had been calling the office and Tabitha kept saying I was unable to take calls. I did tell her to hold my calls, but he should have called my cell phone."

"Did he say if he talked to Raq though?"

"Yes, he said that he spoke with him briefly and that he is on his way to meet with him, and Jon. Noble is coming to pick me up at six and we can get more information then."

Noble was really different, and this scares me. Why is he so worked up? He was upset. I understand I didn't let him know I left work early but it's the response for me that has me wondering.

"Virgie, I really wonder why Mari was referred to me as a client in the first place. She had a misdemeanor domestic battery case where she kicked Shenine in the stomach. Shenine suffered no bodily injuries and refused to press charges. Any criminal attorney could have represented her. I have been racking my brain trying to figure out was this the plot and plan from the beginning to destroy me."

"Girl, why would you think that? You didn't know her or her hoe before this case, right. They are fucked up and that's says a lot."

"I don't know but I have reached out to Albert for some answers." Albert is a good lawyer. Natasha Janine is right when she says anyone could have taken that case so I'm now wondering, why her also?

We both were able to make this day productive. Natasha Janine seems to be turning herself around. She was on the phone with clients, attending several video conference meetings, and reassured her receptionist that she would be in the office tomorrow. I had to use her desktop to handle several pressing matters. It felt a little nostalgic. It is as if we are back in college working on our assignments.

When we attended law school, we always worked in the same room even if we were working on different assignments. We worked well together because we give each other space. This is the reason I like working in an open space because it reminds me of being with my bestie. I love this girl. I will help her get through this, I promise, she will get through this.

I feel my cellphone vibrating. Noble is texting my phone. "I'm here!" This is strange. He never texts, "I'm here." When he normally picks me up, he would call to tell me he is outside. He would either come inside to get me or meet me at the door.

"I'm here," implies to me that he wants me to come out the house. Now I'm really confused if that's the case. He has never asked me to come out before. He is a gentleman. I text, "Okay!" He has me fucked up if he thinks I am some school age girl happy her boyfriend pulled up.

Noble replies, "Are you coming out?" Oh, hell no! He has lost his damn mind. So, I reply, "I sure am! So, I will see you when you come to the door!" What the fuck is going on?

My cell phone is vibrating and it's him.

"Babe, can you please come out? I don't want to talk to Natasha Janine about this shit with her and Raq? You know if I come to the door that's what she is going to ask." "Noble, you are a grown ass man. If you don't want to talk about it, then just tell her. You said when it's about us then it's about us. I would not dare ask you to run out the building so I can avoid your friend."

"Virgie, this shit with them is fucked up and I really want to stay out of it. Babe, I'm at the door now…"

I interject and say, "Then knock on the damn door!" I end the call. What the fuck is really going on? I am the last to know. All of their asses make me sick.

I hear Natasha talking to Noble. I gather my bag and can hear them joking in the dining area. I walk into the room and say, "Girl, let me take this man home. We were up late last night and out all day. He just said how tired he is," he hasn't said shit, but I will cover for him this time, but he will tell me what the fuck is going on.

"Babe, I'm good!" I give him the evil eyes and frowned face like "shut the hell up" and he has the nerve to laugh. I really believe he is losing his damn mind.

"Well Noble, I'm tired so let's go home." He hopped his ass up really quick after I said that. He knows I'm not playing, let's go now!

Natasha Janine knows me too well. I'm sure she senses something is not quite right. She gives me a hug and whispers, "I love you sister. Thank you for today, I couldn't have made it productive without your help and corny jokes." I tell her I love her too and then I follow behind Noble as he exits the door.

Noble and I are walking to my car. "Noble, why are you driving my car? Where is your truck?"

"I let Raq use it." I can't wait until we get in this car. Why the fuck would he give Raq his truck?

I don't even let him close the door completely before I demand answers to my questions, "What the fuck is going on? Why the fuck did you have an attitude earlier on the phone? Why are you afraid to talk to Natasha Janine? Why the fuck would Raq need to drive your pickup truck?"

"Babe, I just want to go home, and I will tell you everything then." This man…. this man!

The ride to the condo is taking forever. We have not uttered a word! Noble gets out of the car and start walking to the elevator. I open the door to get out and say, "I guess you have forgotten about that whole disclaimer you gave me, "Babe, let me open the door when you are riding with me. Those couple of seconds in time will not make a difference but you're rushing out of this truck, can," mimicking the way he said it to me with my nose flared while rolling my eyes.

Noble runs back to the car and says, "Babe, please forgive me! This shit has got me fucked up and it's not even my shit."

"What shit are you talking about? This has to be bigger than I can imagine because you have become undone." What the fuck is going on?

Noble grabs my hand and stops in the middle of the garage.

"Raq is a fucked-up guy who does a lot of fucked up shit!"
There is no need to convince me otherwise.

"Noble, but this isn't new information. Tell me what's going
on and tell me now!"

"Babe, Raq has a camera in his home. He records everything
including his sexual escapades amongst other things. He recorded
the one with Natasha Janine and the ladies.

But on that same particular video, Raq recorded a conversation
he had with a lawyer. The conversation was about a contract he is
seeking that is under investigation. Raq doesn't tell people about
the cameras but Shenine found out about it somehow."

"What's so fucked up about that?" This is Chicago and shit like
this happens all the time that's not a big deal.

"The lawyer came over to his place for one of his wild parties.
Shenine and Mari drugged the lawyer probably to steal
something. They had nonconsensual sex with him while Raq was
having sex with some other ladies in another room."

"Okay, I still am having trouble figuring out what's so fucked
up about this."

"Babe, the lawyer is Albert Ronald! He is running for…."

I immediately interject and say, "Noble, I know who he is!
Natasha Janine and I are friends with him. He is a lead counsel for
one of the largest corporations in this state, this is fucked up!"

"I told you!" This is so bad.

"Noble, he is the person who asked Natasha Janine to take the
case of Mari Corine. Albert knew this bitch wasn't to be trusted
and involved Natasha in this shit. This is so bad!" We proceed to
get on the elevator and ride in complete silence. We both know
how fucked up this is. This can, will, and has the potential to
destroy a lot of people. Those bitches are awful. They are truly
fucked up and fucking up everything that comes in their mist. I

really hate those bitches. What's wrong with fucking someone and moving on if it doesn't work? This is fucked up for real.

As I sit on this couch and Noble is preparing something to eat, I'm thinking to myself about this day. How am I going to tell Natasha Janine that Albert used her because he too was being used? Of all of the people we have worked with, why did Albert seek out Natasha Janine? This is fucked up. Now both of my friends are involved with these bitches and Raq stupid ass. I have no sympathy for his ass. I bet his ass wasn't in another room but sitting right there. He is lying, I bet he is definitely lying trying to make himself the victim. Noble interrupts my thoughts and says, "Babe, Raq wasn't in the room and he is not lying about it."

"Noble, I don't believe his ass!" He shouldn't believe his ass either.

"Babe, we saw the video." Shut the damn door, they saw it. Wait a minute!

"Who the hell is the "they" you are talking about?" We better not be here again with that "we" and "they" shit. I need some names!

"I told you that Jon and I were going to meet Raq." Thank goodness the "they" is him and Jon because I was about to go the hell off.

"Can you just give me the whole story and not bits and pieces?"

"Okay, I finally called Raq back. He told me that he had just finished talking to you. He started off asking me all these damn questions about have you talked to Natasha Janine and did I know what's going on. I told him to tell me what he needed to talk to me about or fuck it. He said that he called Jon and they were about to hook up and could I meet them. You see, Raq will fuck some shit up and when he can't get me then he calls Jon. So, I told him I would meet them. I then called Jon who asked me to pick him up. Jon has a soft spot for Raq's shit, and I don't. When

I'm done listening to Raq's shit, I'll bounce. Jon will stay there listening, so he rode with me. He didn't want to guilt himself into staying if I leave. I learned over time that if Raq called Jon then it some bad shit. Jon tells me that Shenine and Mari stole some video tapes from Raq and there is some shit on them that can't get out."

"But you called acting all crazy on your way to meet Raq. Why were you acting so strange? If this is the normal behavior for his ass?"

"Because Jon and I both have been over his house for some of those wild parties. We would get fucked up over there and no telling what the fuck we all have done on those tapes."

"Are you trying to tell me, there is some video footage out there of Mr. Noble?" I can't wait to hear this.

"Well, I thought I was going to have to tell you that but that's not the case."

"Raq just had the cameras installed in his home about six months ago after Daryl's mom wouldn't stop harassing him." I knew his ass was Daryl's father.

"Raq is the friend you told me about last week. Why am I not surprised?"

"Ms. Lady, one story at a time. We met Raq at the clubhouse at the golf course. He is sitting on the patio on the phone when we walked up. He asked us to give him a minute to finish the call. After he ended the call, he tells us that Shenine came to his home after she was grazed by a bullet in your building begging him for a place to stay." These bitches are full of shit.

"Raq let her stay with him and promised her he would get her an apartment. Well, he came home early last week and found her and Mari fucking in his bed." I'm not surprised by none of it. But why is Raq surprised by their behavior? Noble says that's what they do.

"Babe, as wild as Raq maybe he has this thing about people in his bed. I know it sounds crazy, but he does. He believes his master bed is for his wife. He will not sleep with anyone in it."

"Noble, you are trying to tell me that this damn man has morals. I don't believe none of it."

"Babe, it's not what you believe, it's what he does. He sleeps in another part of his home and tells women that his wife died in that room in that bed."

"This mother fucker tells people, your story. Wow, he is despicable. Wow! This shit doesn't bother you that he uses something so personal to you as an excuse to keep women out of his bed. He is a real piece of shit."

"Of course, I don't like it but I am a man first. I will never tell another man, "stop using my tragedy as your excuse," he knows that it's fucked up."

"Noble, I would cut his ass off. He wouldn't be my friend, but you can finish the story." His despicable ass.

"Babe, Raq is fucked up and there is no escaping that forgone conclusion, but he is still my friend. Let me finish this story because you are turning me on, with your, feisty sexy self." He then leans in and kisses me. I love kissing these lips. I missed "this" Noble today so fuck this story.

"Noble, tell me later. I need you, right now, right at this moment."

It is hot and heavy all in a matter of minutes. I'm sitting on Noble's lap trying to suck his lips off of his face. He is over here pulling away like he doesn't like it.

"What's wrong?"

"I love you! And I don't want this shit with Raq to interfere with that."

"It won't! We will not allow anything to dictate to us how we are to love. We are in control of what we need. So, let's stop talking and get back to the making us feel like us again."

Thursday

Noble picks me up and carries me to the bed. He lays me down and is standing over me.

But this time I am not shying away. I am lying here proud while smiling all "seductively." I'm looking him straight in his eyes and immediately begin rubbing my breasts. I feel like, he wants this. He wants me to delight in myself. He wants to watch, oh now I see. I then start undressing, first my blouse. I am unfastening my buttons, one at a time. With each opening, I softly massage the exposed area. This is quite arousing, let me close my eyes while I do this, so I don't chicken out. I know I can be kind of awkward with my movement when I'm trying to be coy and seductive at the same time.

I have opened every single button on this blouse. Now, I lay here on this bed in my lace bra with these full breasts, ready to be suckled. I squeeze my left breast then my right. This feels so good. I have touched myself thousands of times, but this right here seems so different. I decide to keep this bra on because today I wore my matching lace set. Did he notice it when I got dressed this morning? Is this the reason he wants me to undress myself? We are normally in the thick of it by this time. He never knows what I have on under my clothes because he is peeling them off so fast.

I grab the waistband of my pants and slide my hands along the inside of them. I pull at the button and slowly unfasten it. He doesn't budge an inch and continues to stand there just looking. I know he is delighting in it, but I wonder why he isn't touching me. So, I unzip my pants exposing thee lace panties. I rub my hand over the top. I take my hand and slide it inside my panties so I can feel the top of the smooth skin. I place my right foot on top of his muscle making sure my toes are rubbing up against it. I then take my hands and slide my pants off revealing my new Chantilly lace set.

Houston, I have a problem, Noble lights up like a Christmas tree. He is well pleased. I think it is because even though these are panties. They are a full lace design except for between my legs making them crotchless. We have movement now. It's like he was welcomed home. This man, this easily aroused man.

Noble pulls me to the end of the bed. I start explaining to him what I need. It was important to me at this moment to reiterate to him that our needs are the same.

"Can I be closer to you, Noble? Can I come so close to you that when your heart aches, I may feel it too? As one body, can your affection for me be tightened by your grip? May the force of your grip travel straight to my heart. May it bind the passion we share. May it always cause unrest to the things that try to disturb our love. May we forget what is perceived to be perfect. Allowing us to only to focus on the things that make us uniquely different. May the soliloquies we exhibit always speak to the depth of our love for each other. May they have us to love one another like we are all that matters. May it never push us far, where we can't find our way home. May it confuse our normalcy, distracts our present, and rattles our future. So that we never become complacent. May I meet you where you are. Up, around, and through the things that makes your love so special…"

Noble stops me in the mist of my speaking to comply in the only way he knows how to honor all of my requests. He is soft and so gentle as he pulls me into his embrace. Our body connects like magnets to metal. We are one with each other. We are moving slowly but together. I can feel the sweat from his chest drip off onto me. Even though we are slowly and methodically thrusting our bodies together, it requires a great deal of intensity.

Noble lifts me up so I may sit on his lap as I receive all that he gives. I lean back creating this arch along my body. He says, "Babe, I love this extension, oh I love you everything about you." I continue leaning back holding unto his legs. I am in control. I control the tempo of this pace. This control is what I need. Yes, it's my power he seeks and it's my power he will receive. I feel the euphoria of this encounter wishing it never ends. The next thing I feel is tears leaving my eyes. Why am I crying? I'm not in pain but I can't explain this feeling.

"Babe, what's wrong? Are you okay?" Noble says as he lifts me up and stops this sensual encounter.

"I have no idea. I just started crying."

"Babe, you scare me when you do this?" He says as he looks into my eyes. I want to tell him what's going on, but I don't know. I'm so emotional right now. I start weeping. I'm sitting on his lap straddling him crying like a baby. Noble is rubbing my back as he holds me tight.

"Babe let it all out. You are in the grasp of big strong arms. Whatever it is, we will get through this. Oh babe, I love you so much and I'm hurting because you are hurting." I just continue crying and never say a word. What the hell is wrong with me? What is happening to me? Is this, right here, too much for me?

Are all of these soliloquies taking their toll on me? Are these everyday adventures wearing me down? I want to know; I need to know. I'm losing my control and my power seems to be diminishing. Is Noble, my kryptonite? I collapse in his arms. Noble leans back onto the bed. He is still holding me in his arms, never letting me go.

FRIDAY

I am awakened by Noble getting out of the bed.

"What time is it?" It has to still be late.

"Babe, it's 6:06." We slept through the night straight into the morning. Why is Noble up so early? I am always the first to get up.

"Noble, why are you up so early?" He never gets up before me.

"I need to meet Raq to get my truck." This early, I wonder why he needs to get his truck at this time of the morning.

"Oh, yeah I forgot about that. You didn't get to finish telling me the story. Can you finish now?"

"Babe I will finish later. I need to get with this guy before his day gets started. Knowing him like I do, he will get lost with my shit."

"Okay! Do you want me to drive you over there?" I know he is trying to avoid me going but I'm going anyway. That's why he is up early. He was trying to sneak out of here on me.

"I can take an Uber, so you don't have to get out of bed. I know, you have to go into the office today. I'm not trying to interfere with a black woman's rest." He has jokes early in the morning. He plays way too much.

"I can drop you off then head into the office. I'm well rested for your information."

"Well, since you are well rested. Can we finish what we started last night? You know, before I stroked you into tears." He is crazy talking about "stroke me into tears." I start laughing because he has never, maybe in his dreams.

"Only if we can do it in the shower so we can get going."

"As you will have me to do it, Ms. Lady." He knows that one of my things right there. Do it as I ask.

92

Friday

We are in the shower creating our own steam. It feels wonderful too. I don't know what happened last night, but whatever it was, it's over now. We are in the thick of it like we never skipped a beat. Noble is doing everything I need right this moment. He is squeezing what needs to be squeezed. He is kissing what needs to be kissed. Suckling what needs to be sucked. And caressing every muscle in my body. This shower reminds me of the rain that was bouncing against our bodies the night we were on the balcony. We are moving with the speed and intensity of the shower jets. And, then it is over. We are dressed and heading to Raq's house.

We pull into his driveway. I noticed that Mari's Malibu is parked in the driveway. I have a photographic memory and I memorized her license plate "M47814A."

"Noble, this motherfucker has these bitches over here. I can't stand his bitch ass. He is a fucking coward."

"Why do you think that?" He is having a brain freeze. He knows I'm a lawyer. I have to remember a whole lot of useless information. It's for job security.

"That's Mari's car! I saw it at Natasha Janine's. You remember I told you about that."

"Yeah, I remember but Babe, I am going to need you to stay in the car."

"Hell no! You are fucking kidding me. I'm going in too. I need to see that bitch. They are fucking with my friend. And I need these hoes to know she is not by herself. They are now fucking with me and I'm the last mother fucker they should be fucking with."

When the car stops, I jump out and sprint to the door before Noble could realize I'm gone. This is not my first time here, so I know where I am going. I have picked Noble up from here a couple of times when we first started dating. He used to always joke around to me and say, "I need to make sure you are not a crazy stalker," so we would meet over here.

Noble and I were playing the game of keeping our addresses from one another. We didn't disclose them until about a month into the relationship. We would meet at Natasha Janine's and Raq's houses when we were traveling somewhere together. It was our way of having someone know what we were doing. I never entered inside of his home before so today will be my first visit.

I ring the doorbell and look directly into the camera so they can see my face. Noble is standing on the porch where I am. He says, "Raq, open the door or I am using my key." That's my man, tell Raq's punk ass.

Raq opens the door and steps to the side. I walk straight through the foyer. This damn house is huge. It doesn't look like it from the outside, but it is a beautiful elaborate mansion. I'm standing in the middle of the floor and I can hear Noble talking to Raq.

"Hello Virgie, welcome to my home." I give him that "fuck you" look but say, "yeah thanks." Fuck him with his bitch ass.

Noble says, "Dude, I need my keys and I need them now." I see what Noble is doing. He wants us to leave before I go off but it's too late, I'm about to go off anyway.

"Raq, why the fuck do you have my sister caught up in this shit with these bitches? I know they are here too because I saw Mari's car parked outside."

"Virgie, they are not here. I'm sorry about all of this, it hurts me that she is caught up in this too."

"Raq, fuck you! This is the type of shit you and these hoes are out here doing. But listen up," I start screaming to the top of my lungs. "You all fucked up this time, you fucked up! This shit won't ride, and she will not lose, trust me bitches, she will not lose." I turned and walked back to my car because I was about to cry. I was not going to let these bitches see me cry.

Friday

I'm sitting in my car waiting for Noble to come out of there before I leave. They will not get my man caught up in this shit too. I should have stayed inside to see if they came out from hiding when they heard me screaming. I know they heard me. I have been sitting in this car for about 15 minutes when I see Noble walk out. Why the hell was he in there so long? I blow my horn so he would know I stayed and waited for him. He looks in my direction. He walks to my car and gets in.

"Why were you in there so long?" He better not tell me that he was in there talking to those bitches.

"Raq's ass was apologizing for everything. He even started crying. I told him it's cool…"

I interject, "No it's not! It's not cool, to have someone else caught up in your shit. Noble, you shouldn't have told him that. That's the shit, that's not cool. You and Jon are treating him like a child. He is a grown man, a fucked up grown man, but a grown man still."

"Babe, I agree but I wanted to get my keys and get the hell out of there so I would have offered him a kidney."

"Did they come out after I left?" I know they did. They were trying to wait until I leave. I'm sure of it.

"No! They weren't there. Mari left her car there and someone poured sugar in her tank so she can't move it." Damn, I am wrong. That rarely happens.

"Someone? Raq's ass did it. He is just that petty." I bet he did with his trifling ass.

"No, Frankie did it."

"Who the hell is Frankie?"

"Frankie is Daryl's mother. She saw the car and poured sugar in the gas tank because she thought Mari is Raq's girlfriend."

"Are you fucking serious? This is an epic day of adventures." Wow, now I know the name of Daryl's mother. I wonder why she

95

is so obsessed with Raq. If he isn't the father of her child, then why stalk him. There is definitely more to that story. I bet Noble has the "more" part too.

"Babe, you go on to work. I will call you later. I'm going to go to the car wash and have my truck cleaned. There is no telling what the hell Raq used it for."

"Okay, I love you and I will call you when I get into the office." I say after I kiss him. This man is my Noble being all Noble! I'm driving to my office. I call Natasha Janine to see if she is actually coming into the office too.

"Hey girl! How are you?"

"Hey Virg, I'm actually feeling much better. I talked to Twaab last night and she had me laughing too hard. She told me about Dominica and her boyfriend. Zam is a scary motherfucker. I may have to have Zam kick Mari's ass for me." She is definitely feeling better. Twaab has that way with people. She can turn everything around instantaneously.

"Girl, I just left Raq's house with Noble," we say it instinctively, "with his bitch ass!" Then we both burst out laughing.

"What did he say Virgie?" I wish I had something to tell her, but I don't.

"Stut, Stut, stuttering, not a damn thing." Liteally, not a damn thing. "Well, Albert called me last night and wants to meet with me this evening."

"Really?" She is going to snap when she finds out what he did.

"Do you want me to go with you?"

"Girl, why would I need you to come with me to this meeting with Mr. Albert? I can handle his ass on my own. We are just meeting so he can tell me why the fuck he passed this bitch off to me. But, let me get off this phone. I lost my security pass. I need to show Manuel my ID to get into the building." We end the call.

This will be bad. When she finds out what he did to save himself, she is going to tear him a new one. I'm glad she is coming into the office. Fuck that hiding out shit. Face their asses with a straight face so they will know you are not playing with them. I stand firmly on that principle.

I'm parked and walking into the office. As I enter my office, I notice a beautiful woman sitting in the waiting area. I make eye contact with her and say, "Good morning!" She replies, "Good morning," with a British accent. I immediately notice it; I love how British people sound. I then walk to Tabitha's desk and say, "Good morning, Tabitha!"

"Good morning Ms. Kelly. Your 9:30 appointment is here. Do you need me to get you something before your meeting?" She knows I like tea before I have a meeting. It helps me to relax before I start talking business with people.

"No Tabitha, I am good. If the file is in my office or if you placed it there, I should be fine. Allow me a couple of minutes to settle into the office, review the file, and I will call you when I'm ready."

"Sure, Ms. Kelly!" I didn't even check my schedule. It is a good thing I came into the office. I hate when I have appointments and I am not prepared. Let me review the file and get this day started.

I walk into my office. I see a large file on my desk. The client is Francline Waylon. She is suing Roscoe Langley for a breach of contract. As I read this case file, I can tell this case is going to be a whole mess. This woman is suing her previous partner for breach of contract. They were business partners on an acquisition contract for some commercial real estate.

Mr. Langley secured the deal without Ms. Waylon. She is suing him for 1.5 million dollars for pain, suffering, and breach of contract. One of her demands is to have him submit to a paternity exam by an independent physician. The results of the exam will be revealed in a sealed envelope only to the respective attorneys. I don't know what the hell is going on here, but I am not sure I will be taking this case. One of the partners referred this client to me because of the dollar amount.

My company investigates all claims before setting up a consultation to ensure our time is not wasted when meeting with clients. Ms. Waylon's claim is legitimate, but it just may be too much for me. I will meet with her first before I send it to another attorney. I can really use the money from the attorney fees, but do I really want the headache I believe will be associated with this case.

"Tabitha, I am ready for Ms. Waylon." I'm going to make this quick.

I hear Tabitha informing her I am ready to see her. Then Tabitha opens the door and announces the client. I stand up and extend my hand out to her.

"Good morning, Ms. Waylon. I am Attorney Virgie Mae Kelly. Please have a seat."

"I reviewed your case file. Is there any other information you would like to share regarding this claim?"

"Ms. Kelly, your reputation precedes you. I tried for years to seek your services for this matter. However, this law firm standards are unmatched." There is no lie in that statement. Every detail and all documents must be verified. This is why we are well sought out because if the case is taken by this office, we basically guarantee a win. We have lost cases in the past, but our number of judgement wins outweigh the losses. "Ms. Waylon, thank you for your acknowledgment. How can I be of assistance to you?"

"I am here because my former business partner is in breach of our contract. We formed a partnership to acquire commercial real estate around the city of Chicago. I would find the land, develop the relationship with the owner, find points of weaknesses, then hand those over. My former partner would exploit those weaknesses I found to acquire the land. We were in this business for six years.

During that time, I became pregnant with my son. I am not ashamed that I formed a relationship with my partner. And from that relationship, I gave birth to a beautiful son. He always denied being the father. He was adamant about having a paternity test conducted so I complied. I was confident that the test results would prove he was the father. So, after years of him requesting it and hearing his lies about this being for the sake of the child, I agreed to the test.

Keep in mind, I continued our partnership until I heard him on the phone one day with his friend. I overheard him thanking his friend for assisting him in obtaining the test results. I believe he even went so far as to have that friend to falsify the results. My son was seven at this time. This was the same year that he acquired this multimillion-dollar deal. I secured initially. I was not included in the final closure of the deal and my former partner took extreme measure to keep me away.

I was later issued a restraining order stating to stay away from him. He stated that I was harassing him and threatening his safety. All of my documents were destroyed. My name and reputation were slandered. As a result, I took a manager position in a strip club. I was forced to be estranged from my son and family for years. Nevertheless, I stayed persistent in my pursuit to get back everything that was taken from me. My methods have been extreme but there the methods I chose to use. I have done everything in my power to seek closure in this matter, but he refuses to meet with me. I want what is owed to me and for him to be a father to my child. I recently learned that I only had ten years before the statute of limitations of my claim expires. And, I have reached the end of that term. What I want is? For Raq to pay and I mean pay dearly."

I know this lady did not say "Raq." Did she just say "Raq"? What the hell?

"Ms. Waylon, is your case against Roscoe Langley?" Raq's damn name is Roscoe Langley. No wonder he tells people his name is Raq. Roscoe Langley sound like a name for a prestigious businessman. There is nothing left to the imagination from that name.

"Yes, Ms. Kelly. My case is against Roscoe "Raq" Langley who is Noble's best friend." Aww, hell No! I am definitely not taking this case. This damn lady can't be serious. So, this is "Frankie"? Daryl's mother? The lady who worked for wages. The stalker? The crazed woman who poured sugar in Mari's gas tank. Oh, hell no! What the fuck? How does this lady even know me?

"Ms. Waylon, thank you for seeking the assistance of our law office." It appears that this case cannot be represented by me due to the conflict of interest for all parties involved. I must decline and ask her to leave my office after I get more information.

"You mentioned Noble who is best friends with Mr. Langley. Can you elaborate on your relationship with Noble?" This better not be another fucked up relationship someone had with Noble. Please let there be another Raq and Noble. Please Lord!

"Ms. Kelly, I have tried for years to get you or this firm to represent me regarding this matter. You were the attorney on a case where my friend was sued by a restaurant for violating a NDA. You and your client won the case and that was when I decided I needed to have you represent me." Wait a minute, she damn well, not know Kelle's ass too. I interject, "What is the name of the restaurant?"

"It was Wells Delicious Popcorn Shop." Thank God! I did win that one. The case took every ounce of fight I had in me. My client was terrible, but they were the true owners of the recipe.

"Ms. Waylon, please excuse my interruption. You were saying?"

"I would come to this office building often in hopes of catching you coming into the building. Last month, I came to schedule this appointment and when I arrived, I saw Dr. Winston dropped you off in front of the building. He walked you to the door and gave you a kiss. Dr. Winston is Raq's best friend. He is a wonderful man who provided angel funding for my son. My son is now in his first year of college and aspires to be a doctor like Dr. Winston."

"If you have observed Dr. Winston and I then you should know I cannot represent you in this civil matter. It would be a direct conflict of interest and jeopardize you in receiving a fair trial."

"Well, I'm not very familiar with the law. I just know that I wanted the best lawyer for the job. It is my belief you are that person."

"If you would like I can pass your case to another attorney in this office. I'm sorry I can't be of any assistance. I wish you good luck in your endeavors."

"Thank you, Ms. Kelly. Would I need to have another consultation regarding my matter? It took a month to get this appointment and again I'm near the end of my term."

"If you can wait in the waiting area, I will contact my partners and see if someone could meet with you today. I will have my receptionist work on it now."

After this meeting, I am hitting myself in the head. This can't be real. I can see Francline "Frankie" sitting there nervously. She is drop dead gorgeous. Noble never mentioned how beautiful she was. It is a damn shame when people describe someone, they always point out the unattractive attributes.

This lady looks like she could have whatever man, she wants. Damn, and she still wants Raq's ass. I see where Daryl gets his looks from. I have so many questions. Raq is exactly who I thought he is, his despicable ass. My phone is ringing and it's Noble. Damn, I forgot to call him when I got into the office.

"Hey baby!" How am I going to tell him about Frankie? That would be a direct breach of attorney client privilege. I wonder is this why she sought me so I couldn't tell them. She is going to kill Raq in court. She has him by the balls. I'm so surprised he has that amount of money. I would have never imagined that he was that well off. Noble said that his friend came into some wealth. Now I have some context about this story.

"Babe, you didn't call me and let me know you made it to the office."

"I'm sorry. When I arrived I had a consultation scheduled. You know, how I am when I haven't prepared. How is your day going?"

"So far so good. I'm meeting Daryl for lunch. He wants to talk to me about something. I will be downtown, if you would like for me to drop something off to you. I would love to taste those lips. I miss you!" This man's voice even drives me wild. I love me some Noble.

I am swamped with work. I haven't paid any attention to time. It's 11:09. I should call Noble to bring me something to eat. Before I could dial his number, he is calling me.

"Noble, I was just thinking about you."

"Virgie, are you meeting with Frankie? Daryl told me that his mother has an appointment with you today. Were you going to tell me that? What the hell is going on? Why would she be meeting with you? Is she there now? This is fucked up!"

"Noble, slow down. What are you talking about? I am not at liberty to disclose to you, who or what I am discussing with my clients or any potential clients. Don't ever call my office questioning me about my clients, my job duties, and my responsibility to you as your girlfriend as it is relating to my job!" This man has the nerve to question my actions. I have tons of questions about his actions, his friends, and all of these damn secrets surrounding all of them. And let him tell it, "he isn't ready to disclose," so he better shut the hell up talking to me.

"I'm sorry babe, you're right, that's your job and how dare I question what you are doing. I sincerely apologize. Daryl wanted to talk to me about his future plans for school and mentioned that his mom was going to see you."

"How is Daryl? He is doing good, but he is concerned about his mother. He thinks she is up to something. He said that she is hanging with some unsavory women from the strip club. Babe, please get back to work and I will see you later. I'm sorry again. I love you!"

I really need a drink. It's not even noon and I am tired as fuck.

"Tabitha, can you step into my office?"

"Yes, Ms. Kelly?"

"Tabitha, close the door. Did you find someone to take Ms. Waylon's case?"

"Yes, Ms. Kelly. Mr. Simpson is currently meeting with her now."

"That's great. If anyone other than me can secure a victory it would be Chester Simpson. I'm happy about that. I saw yesterday that Noble was speaking to you. What was he saying?" She better tell me if she wants to keep this job. I pay her salary. I hope she knows that.

"Noble, asked if I knew your ring size. I informed him that I didn't. He wanted to know if there was some way, I could obtain it for him. I told him that I would try but it would be better to just ask you and he said he would." Oh my God! He is serious about spending the rest of his life with me. Wow! I can't say I'm ready though. This will be the first time someone proposed to me. Tabitha took the surprise out of it. I should have never inquired. I have a way of fucking things up. Damn, I'm so nosey. Damn, damn, damn!

My workday has finally come to an end. I can go and sit down somewhere. I should call Natasha Janine to see how her day is going.

"Hey Girl, how is your day going?"

"It's finally over. I'm wrapping up now to get out of here. I just realized why I hate missing a day at work. I return and they are giving me the worst cases ever. They think because I'm black I should handle all of these dang crazy ass cases from the hood." I know what she means because they do the same thing here.

"I'm leaving too. My day has been equally crazy. Girl, please make sure you call me after you meet with Albert. I am dying to know what his reason for doing you, like this is."

"I will! I'm having Twaab and Zam meet me there in case Albert says something that warrants him to get his ass kicked and you know Zam Will do it." We both start laughing. She isn't wrong. Zam takes his unresolved issues out on anyone who is brave enough to receive them.

I hope Albert tells her what I already know about this shit. I don't want to tell her what Noble told me. To think that he is entangled in this shit is mind blowing. Albert is so damn bogus for what he did to my bestie. Natasha Janine use to have a crush on him. He loved him some Natasha Janine too, but it didn't work out for some reason or another. He is smart, charismatic, handsome, and has a great smile. I'm not surprised that he is a freak. Those are the kind of guys who usually are freaks, those unassuming type. But I'm curious to know how he even knows Raq trifling ass.

Instead of driving to Noble, I feel a need to get some chicken wings from the hood. This day was so crazy. I need to go drive over on the Westside and grab me six wings with mild sauce. Noble hates eating greasy food, so I don't even have to worry about asking him if he wants something. I can spend this time alone, enjoying my food, and listening to the soundtrack to the movie Sparkle. Aretha sang her heart out in those songs.

I pull up to the restaurant. I see Cheryl mean ass is here too. She drives a grey Range Rover with personalized license plate that says, "L84C8," which explains everything. I'm just hating, it's the name of her company. She owns a bakery called Late for Cake. I'm really surprised to see her here. I thought she was too bougie to be eating wings in the hood the way she acted at Kelle's birthday dinner party.

His Aunt Diane threw him a dinner party at her house in Beverly. She invited all of us including Mr. Sid, my Auntie, Cheryl, Nuri and myself. It was a surprise party, and my job was to bring Kelle. It was a total mess. Cheryl knew I was supposed to bring Kelle to the party, but she was determined not to let that happen like he was still her husband. She called him all morning about nonsense. She would say, "Nuri wants to have breakfast with you, Nuri wants to take you shopping for a gift, Nuri wants to have lunch with you." This bitch even called the night before saying, "Nuri asked if you would stay the night so she can wake you up on your birthday." Kelle's ass wasn't having none of that, he wanted to wake up lying next to me. He told her, "No baby, Daddy promised Ms. Virgie he would spend this birthday with her." When I say Cheryl was mad, she was big mad! She was at Aunt Diane's complaining about everything. My Auntie got so mad and started cursing her out. It was to the point that I ended up taking her home before she kicked Cheryl's ass. Auntie doesn't play about her niece. She knew Cheryl was trying to ruin it for me.

I walk into the restaurant and notice the guy Cheryl is with. It's the new guy that works at Noble's building. Wow! Cheryl is an old cougar. She is standing there laughing loudly rubbing his face. The young man immediately straightens up and greets me. "Hello, Ms. Kelly!"

"Hello, you!" I say stuff like this when I can't remember people's name.

"Hey Cheryl, I see you are out here in the hood. I never would have thought you like wings and fries."

"Hello Virgie, for your information I do like wings and fries. I am here with Carter. His family owns this restaurant."

She sounds dumb as hell. She is standing up here bragging on some second-generational wealth when she is a successful businesswoman. Whatever, I could care less.

"Virgie, I guess you are here to pick up some fried chicken wings for your man?"

"No, I'm picking some up for myself." I really wanted to say, "No bitch, I'm picking some up for your ex-husband, but I don't have time for her today.

"Carter, I haven't seen you at the condominium."

"Yeah, I was let go after I let a delivery guy in without the permission of the resident."

"Really, why would you do that?"

"The gentleman said that the resident was expecting him and there was no need to call the unit."

"Well, I'm sorry to hear that. Good luck to you and I wish you much success in your endeavors."

I look at Cheryl and say, "Cheryl," then proceed to the counter. Fuck Cheryl with her mean ass.

Friday

I'm sitting in my car eating my wings and listening to my jams. I am interrupted when Kelle calls my phone. Cheryl probably called him and told him she saw me. I'm not answering his call. Let his ass go to voicemail, I will check the message later. Damn, his ass is calling again. Why can't he just leave me alone? I don't want to be bother with him. Really Kelle? He is calling again.

"Hello!" If this call is about his random calling shit, I swear I'm going off.

"Virgie, why aren't you answering? Sid fell and hurt himself."

"Where is he? Did you call my aunt?"

"He came by my place. He doesn't want me to call her. Can you come over here and help me talk him into going to the hospital? I can't stay here because I need to go to the restaurant." Kelle and this damn restaurant shit. Why does he need to go to the restaurant after it has closed anyway?

"Kelle, I will not be able to do that. Let me speak to Mr. Sid. I will try to get him to go to the hospital."

"Here he is."

"Mr. Sid, what happened? Kelle tells me you fell and hurt yourself. Do you want to go get examined?"

"Hey, my sweet Virgie, I'm in a little pain but it's nothing I can't handle."

"Mr. Sid, pain doesn't have to be handled. Do you want me to come and take you to the hospital and get checked out?"

"Sweetie, I will be good. But can you take me home so Kelle can go to the restaurant?"

"Sure, I'm on my way."

This story is not making any sense to me. I'm going to call my Auntie. She answers on the first ring like she was expecting my call.

"Hey Auntie, how are you feeling?" If something is going on, she will tell me.

"Hey baby, I was just about to call you." Call me? I wonder about what.

"What's wrong?"

"Child, it's Sid ass. He done ran his ass out of here and fell down the stairs."

"Really, Kelle just called me to convince him to go to the hospital. I'm on my way to pick him up."

"Don't pick his ass up, let him stay there."

"Why? What happened?" She is upset for real.

"Child, I'm sick of their asses. He and Kelle can stay together!" I'm not surprised by that statement. They are thick as thieves. Kelle's ass has something to do with this.

"Auntie, tell me what happened."

"You know Kelle does nothing but uses Sid ass. He is underpaying him, playing him, and sending his ass on these rescue missions. Kelle called Sid a couple of nights ago to go somewhere with him. When he came over last night, I was curious about where they went. So, you know me I asked his ass. He told me that they went to Cheryl's boyfriend's job to spy on Cheryl."

"Spy on Cheryl? Wow, Cheryl hangs out at her boyfriend's job."

"Child, I don't know. Sid said while they were sitting in the lobby that Noble walked in."

"Noble?" Noble is going to kill Kelle's ass.

"Yes, your Noble! I told Sid, y'all asses are spying on my baby and that shit isn't cool. He tells me that Cheryl is dating some young ass boy who works there. She saw you one day she was there to pick him up and told Kelle about it. She was trying to make him jealous. Sid said that Kelle didn't pay it any mind until you and Natisha's ass came to the restaurant last week."

"Auntie her name is Natasha Janine." I don't know why I corrected her. She is going to go off.

Friday

"Virgie, I don't give a damn what her name is because you know who the hell, I'm talking about. Now let me finish telling you this shit." This lady has no patience. I guess that's where I get it from.

"Sid said Noble called for a delivery order in last week and when it was prepared. Kelle told Sid that was where your boyfriend lived. Sid said that Kelle really wanted to handle the delivery, so he made like he was overwhelmed at the restaurant and needed him there. Kelle told the delivery guy to make sure he canvassed the apartment when the door opened to see if a woman was there. He told him that his sister dates this guy and he wanted to know if she was over there. The delivery guy told Kelle when he returned that he saw a purse near the door but didn't see her. I told Sid that he should have told me this from the beginning instead of playing me for information."

"Auntie, how did Mr. Sid get hurt if you all were just talking."

"Because I heard him on the damn phone trying to tell Kelle he told me everything. I went the hell off, and I may have grabbed my bat and threatened to bust his head. I can't recall all of the details about that part at this time." She remembers and did just that. This lady, this lady doesn't play about her family.

I pull up at Kelle's. He's already gone. I call Mr. Sid and asks if he needs help. He declines but then comes out limping pretty badly. He probably does need medical attention, but Auntie said, "bring him over here to me." I helped him into the car.

"Mr. Sid, Auntie wants me to bring you to her place."

"Sweetie, no just take me home. Your aunt is trying to kill me. I'm sure she told you what I did."

"She isn't trying to kill you. Kelle's ass is the one trying to get you killed. He is all up in my business. Noble is going to hurt him. If you are with him when he does, he is going to hurt you too. Now I can take you home or to her, but you have to decide."

109

"Okay, take me to my baby." I know that's right Mr. Sid. Go home to the woman that loves you.

I dropped Mr. Sid off at Auntie's. He was saying that he was hungry. Kelle didn't give him anything to eat. I am so tired that I just shared my wings. I am not about to drive anywhere else. I want and need to go home.

I call Noble. I just realized; I haven't talked to him since earlier.

"Hello Mr. Noble!"

"Hey babe, are you still in the office?" I don't want to have this Kelle discussion on the phone.

"I'm on my way to your place."

"Good, I miss you. I'm walking around this place, smelling all of your things."

"You nasty!" He is probably talking about my panties. This may be his thing too.

"Nasty for you. What's your ETA?" I know what he is trying to do he wants me to give him a time so he can get some idea of where I am.

"I'm just leaving my Auntie's house. I should be there soon."

"Babe, can you squeeze your pillows? They need to know I miss them too."

"Noble, they know." It is too hot out here. I don't want to drive to his place all hot and bothered. But this man knows I will do it. I grab my left breast and start rubbing it on top of my shirt.

"Babe, take your right hand and stick it inside your bra, rub your nipple softly then place it between your finger and gently squeeze." As I do as he says, I am at a red light on Ogden Avenue. I notice a man selling newspapers in the street. He hears and sees what I am doing too. I'm so embarrassed.

"Noble, if you want these pillows, then don't be lazy and have me to play with them.

You're going to have to do the work to show them how much they mean to you."

"Babe, what work will I have to do? Please tell me. If I'm working on them, then you would be home having me playing with them. They wouldn't have wanted to leave me.

Do I need to come and get them?"

"You are invited to come."

"Babe, is this a real invitation or are we still playing make believe?"

"You would have to wait until I am there and see." I love our flirting banter.

As I am attempting to unlock the door to the condo, the door swings open. Noble didn't even let me put my key into the lock before he opens it. He pulls me in and wraps me up in his arms ever so sensually. The smell of him is so mesmerizing. He is wearing my favorite cologne. He immediately rubs his hands all over my body, as if he has forgotten how I feel. He then squeezes my cushion and says, "Oh how I missed you so! Don't stay away so long. I need you here with me. I need to touch you to prove to myself I'm not dreaming. I need your touch. I need to kiss your neck. I need to touch these thighs," as he carries me straight to the bedroom.

"Noble, after a day like today. I am going to need for you to show me. A lot happened today, and I just want…." Without allowing me to finish, he interrupts and starts kissing me.

I feel like he is trying to suck my tongue right out of my mouth. The feeling is so arousing that I take his face in my hands because I want him to kiss me forever. He is sucking my lips one by one, my cheeks, my chin, my earlobe, and now my neck. He lays me down on the bed and say, "Babe, I want to taste all of you. Can I do that?"

"You don't have to ask me that." He has done that on more than one occasion. I don't really get the question.

"I do need to ask because I don't want to give you this tonight," holding his penis in his hand while standing directly in front of me.

"I want to suck, nibble, and fondle your body with my tongue. But this will make you desire this," pointing to his penis again.

"Babe, I am going to need you to delight in only the pleasure I will give tonight. So, I ask again, can I taste you?"

This body of mine felt every word he spoke. I am seductively closing my eyes, holding my head back, arching my body, grabbing these sheets, spreading these thighs and then I say, "Delight yourself in every part of my body." And he did!

SATURDAY

It's about 4 o' clock in the morning and I am sore. I'm wrapped in Noble's arms. I move his arm to get up from here. As I walk past the mirror I discover where this soreness is coming from. I have a hickey on each of my breast, on my collarbone, my back, my stomach, on the top of my vagina, on each of my buttocks, and all along my legs. He was a vampire trying to suck the blood out of me. What am I going to do with this man?

I walk into the kitchen and realize that I don't have on any clothes. There are windows on top of windows. I would normally shy away from walking in the nude but not this time. I have a man who loves all of me. He is sweet, considerate, and passionate. And let me not fail to mention he possesses all of the other qualities I need to appeal to my five senses. My man! I sit at the table drinking a glass of wine when Noble walks into the room.

"Babe, are you good? I hope I didn't hurt you."

"Noble, I'm good I needed something to drink so I poured myself a glass of wine." "I see you're feeling yourself. You're out here in my favorite suit. There was a time when you would have never done that. I'm happy you feel free and at home to do it."

"Thanks sweetie, you make me feel like that! I could get use to this too."

"Oh really, I thought if we're to get married we would have to move to your place so I decided that we wouldn't," and he sits in the chair next to me also nude.

"Whatever Noble! Tabitha can't hold water, so she already told me."

"Tabitha told you, what?" He knows what she told me.

"She told me that you wanted my ring size?" He can't deny it. He told her that and she told me.

"Babe, I told her to tell you that. I know your ring size. It is 6 and 3/4. I measured your ring finger when we first spent the night together."

"What? Why would you tell her to tell me that?"

"Really Virgie! You are really asking me that," while he is tilting his head to the side giving me the side eye.

"I told Tabitha to tell you that because I knew you would ask her what I was talking to her about. I was asking her was she single because I thought she would be a good date for Daryl. She is single too. Daryl has been having his share of bad luck in relationships so I thought I would ask."

"Really, you hate when I play matchmaker, but you have the nerve to do it yourself. I don't believe you."

"Well, you make your own decision about what you believe. That's what I did, and you can ask her if you don't believe me. I would want you to be completely surprised when I propose. I wouldn't risk your receptionist giving you the heads up."

"When?" Wait a minute. What is happening here?

"You heard me, when!" He then stands up behind me and massages my shoulders, neck and down the spine of my back.

"How sore are you?" But I'm so captivated by his touches I didn't answer.

"Babe, my muscle needs to enter his home where he can delight all morning long. Can he come in?"

Next thing, I know he is picking me up from behind bending me over the table.

"Shall I moisten your area or are you already moist?" I'm at a loss for words. I want to tell him no, but my body is saying yes so, I have no words to speak. He drops to his knees and moistens all of my area one at a time.

"Babe, I need to enter my home right here right now!" His home? Is this his dwelling? I can feel the thrust of his fingers which makes me grasps for air. Then he makes his presence known, he is at home. I grab the edge of this table, holding on for dear life, stroke after stroke after stroke. He is giving it to me like it's our first time together. Noble is giving me all he has and when I say all, baby I mean everything. And it feels magnificent if I may say.

We are back in bed fast to sleep. I wake up and realize it is 11:09. I begin scurrying out of this bed to get ready.

"Babe, it's Saturday! You don't have to go to work." But I do have other places I visit. "I know, but I have a spa appointment at 1 and I can't be late." This is my "me time" every other week.

"You don't have to leave for that. I can massage that body some more, but I don't believe I left you with any tension."

"Noble, this is my "pamper me" day. I have appointments for hair, manicure, pedicure and waxing."

"Babe, I just waxed that ass!" He has jokes, really Noble. He tried but I really need a waxing seriously though.

"Go back to sleep! What do you have planned today?"

"I might just hang out with the guys since my lady will be getting waxed. Babe, please tell me that a lady is doing the waxing down there.

"Why are you jealous or super protective of this muscle?" Both, but I let him choose one.

"Neither! I left hickeys down there, so I don't want you to be embarrassed."

"Really Noble! Well, it is what it is. I'm already embarrassed." This man!

I made it here in great time. I showered and dressed before Noble could get out of the bed. I normally come every two weeks for my "pamper me" day. I am determined to keep this time for myself. Noble is right. He waxed this ass all night long. I feel goofy for even thinking that, but I will never admit it to him.

115

I walk into the spa. The energy this place is giving me is making me wish I stayed in the bed with Noble. There is a new girl working the receptionist desk. I'm not really surprised by that because there is a high turnover rate at this establishment. The customers are grand and bougie with unrealistic demands. I only come here because I am very protective of the space I share with people. This place encourages isolation because of its clientele. The young lady tells me that after undressing I will be serviced in room 101. I am normally serviced in 201 but when some "high profile" person is here I am moved. I wonder who it is today.

A couple of months ago, the room was given to an actress that they ushered out through the back door. I never inquire because I feel like I'm "high profile" too. They better ask somebody.

I am attorney Virgie Mae Kelly, the best civil attorney ever. Enough already, let me get out of these clothes before I'm late to the room. I step out of the stall after undressing and observes those hickeys on my collarbone, neck and arms. I look like I have been abused. I should have just cancelled this appointment. Shit, I'm a grown woman being sucked and nibbled on by a grown man who I love. Oh, hell no, this bitch is still living! She better not say a damn… And here she goes interrupting my thoughts.

"Hello Virgie! How strange is it to see you here?" Mikki says. This bitch Mikki is here.

She knows damn well I come here often. She is the person who referred me. I hate her ass.

"Yeah, hey Mikki," I say as I am rolling my eyes and flaring my nose at her.

"Virgie, how have you been? Is everything okay? Why are you bruised up? If you ever need to talk to someone I'm always here. I miss you, girl."

"Let's get something straight so we don't have to straighten it out again. Fuck you Mikki with your trifling ass! Don't ever worry about my damn bruises and don't mind my fucking business. If I ever need someone to talk to bitch, it would never be you. Now, get the fuck out of my face."

"Okay Virgie, Kelle was right. You have changed. I will comply with your request. It is time for my appointment in room 201."

"Kelle said, what?" I know this bitch didn't mention Kelle's ass. She is crazy as hell. He can't say shit about me.

"Yes, Kelle hosted an event for me at his restaurant. He shared how you changed. Take care," as she walks into room 201 for her services. Kelle is hosting this scandalous event. He is probably doing it because he knows she is my friend. He is trying to get close to me again.

This bitch is a trip. Now she is fucking around with Kelle. She is probably lying. I can't believe this bitch. She has the money to take my room. I hate her, fucking hoe. Why the fuck is Kelle fucking around with her? It was probably her swinger's event. Her group likes to mingle first before they invite you to the throw down. Oh my, I never told Kelle about the tape. This bitch knows he doesn't know so she is fucking around with me. This is why I hate her ass. She is always on some mind manipulation shit, the whole reason why I thought she was a good lawyer. She is a damn cuckoo bird with her sorry ass. I should have never gotten tied up with her and her shit.

After three hours of pampering, I feel like a new woman. I can't believe that Noble put hickeys on my inner thighs. I must have passed out because I don't recall any of it. My masseuse Jory said, "I see someone was having a great time because these hickeys are parallel to each other. I wanted to die. She is a cool lady, so I didn't need to explain what happen. Jory and I are on our second year together. She even said as I was leaving, "Enjoy your time together but tell him legs are for walking not sucking." I laughed so hard. I can't wait to tell Noble what she said.

My phone is vibrating. "Hey girl, I was just about to call you." It's Natasha Janine. She's surprisingly calm.

"I could meet you at Stella's. Girl, this is a perfect spot to have a drink and talk. I could use a drink. Mikki's ass was at the spa. I have to tell you all about it. How about at 4:30? I just want to check with Noble to see if he scheduled something for us. Hope to see you soon." This is very strange. Why the hell isn't she angry? She is too calm for me. I would be livid if I found out Albert did that shit to me. What if Albert didn't tell her? Well, if she asks me, I'm telling. I need to process this with Noble before I do. I'm going to call him when I get in the car.

"Hello Mr. Noble." I need to tell him about Mikki's ass. Knowing her like I do she will if she sees him.

"Hello Ms. Lady! How was that waxing?" He just wants to know if I had a male esthetician roaming down there.

"Good, but my male esthetician said, stop chewing on me." How does he like that?

"I hope you told him that's your last visit because going forward I will be tending to that area."

"Whatever! My masseuse was the one who had something to say after my massage. She told me to enjoy our time together, but these legs are for walking and not sucking."

"Poor lady, she has been deprived all her life. What are you up to?"

"I am going to meet Natasha Janine at Stella's. She met with Albert Ronald last night."

"Do you think he told her what's going on with Raq?"

"I will find out shortly." I need to check his temperature regarding me telling her.

"She is probably going to ask me if I know anything about it. She is my bestie. I don't want to lie if she does."

"Babe, you don't have to check my temperature about that. I would never ask you to lie for my friend. If I didn't think she should know I would not have told you. You have to make that decision yourself."

"What are you doing?" He is probably smelling my underwear again.

"Right now, or later?" See, I knew it.

"Right now."

"I'm touching myself thinking about those hickeys I left on you." He is so predictable. "Really Noble! You know what, knowing you, yes you really are. What are you doing later?"

"I'm supposed to meet Jon. He wants to talk to me about MJ. He said everything is going great. They are going to church together tomorrow. I told him to be careful. These Kelly girls will have you in the house butt naked playing with yourself waiting for them to come home."

"I can't with you. I need to call MJ to check on her too. I'm happy things are going well for them. I will call you after drinks with Natasha Janine."

I arrived at Stella's. I can see from outside of the window that Natasha Janine is already inside. Stella's is a black owned coffee shop in the west loop. Stella is one of our good friends from college. We love patronizing her. There are only four booths in the coffee shop. Stella's could accommodate a large crowd but took the less is better approach. She prefers a pickup and go crowd and booths require reservations except for us. We have it like that.

I walk into the coffee shop. Natasha Janine and Stella are talking and laughing.

"Hey ladies, how are you all doing?"

Stella says, "Great Virgie! You look great lady. I guess things are going great with your dude, huh."

"Yes Stella, things are going great with my Noble! You are looking equally great yourself. How is Marley?" Marley is her husband. He is a great guy and really cool. "Marley is Marley! You all just missed him. He was manning the shop until I arrived. I was sharing with Natasha Janine we are selling the shop."

"Really, wow! We love it here!"

"Yeah, we are moving to the ATL. Marley got a job to produce a film there."

"Congratulations, I'm so happy for you all." I notice that Natasha isn't laughing like she was when I walked in.

"Sister, are you good?"

"Yeah Virgie, just thinking."

"I will leave you all to talk. It was great seeing you Virgie. You know we will be throwing a big party. Marley wouldn't have it any other way. Hopefully, I will meet Mr. Noble then."

"We will be there, for sure." When Stella walks away from the table, I grab Natasha Janine's hand.

"Girl, what is wrong? What did Albert say?"

She immediately starts crying. I reach out and hug her. "We will get those bitches I promise you that!"

"Virgie, Albert has cancer!" I know this man didn't tell her that. What the fuck? "How do you know? Did he tell you that? Is that why he met with you? Tell me what happened from the beginning because I didn't know he was sick." Wow, he went for the "Oh I'm sick" and this is why I did this to you.

"Virgie, last night when I met Albert at Bricks for drinks. You know me, I always get there early so I can canvas the place out. I don't want any of my clients to see me out drinking. I told Twaab and Zam where I was going. The plan was for me to text them if I needed some support for his ass. I stay ready in case I didn't like what he was saying.

Albert arrived there shortly after me. Girl he looked bad. It took me by surprise because I wasn't used to seeing him so disheveled."

"Is that's why you are saying he has cancer? Because he looked bad."

"Virgie, he told me he has cancer are you going to let me finish the story or not."

"Okay, finish then," she takes forever to tell a damn story. She knows I have no patience.

"He sat down at the table and started crying. I'm saying to myself what the fuck is going on here. He said, "I'm so sorry about what happened to you." Now I'm sitting here like let me pull out my phone to text Twaab, but he kept talking."

"Albert told me that he met Raq at a fundraiser for one of these politicians. He and Raq would see each other in passing when one day Raq called him up. Raq wanted to bounce some ideas off of him regarding some developmental properties. Raq told him he had an inside source who told him about the land. Albert met with him because he was curious to know more. Raq invited him to his place. When he got there, it was some type of freak fest. He wasn't cool with that, but he stayed."

"I bet he did stay." He is a damn freak so that shit was probably right up his alley.

"Let me tell you, damn." She is really testy about Albert's ass.

"Okay I digress." I need to stop it. She is under a lot of stress.

"Albert said he and Raq never got the chance to talk because the house was full of people. So, after that whenever Raq had a party, he would invite Albert. Albert said that about two months ago, Raq had another party. He said something was different about this party because there were only women there and no men. Raq told him to make himself at home. Albert said Raq finally started talking about the developmental properties, but Albert said he didn't feel comfortable discussing it in front of the women.

Raq dipped off into the back of the house with two women. He stayed up front. One girl insisted on making him a drink to get him to relax so he gave in. While he was trying to relax another girl came up and unzipped his pants. She started to suck his dick while the girl who made him a drink walked and put her breast in his mouth. He said the parties are wild but never to this point. He said he eventually passed out and woke up on Raq's couch and discovered that his wallet was missing. A month later, he was contacted by Mari who was arrested and named him as her attorney. He never knew the girl's names until the arrest. Mari told him that Shenine was underage at the time of the incident and if he didn't represent her that she would report him. Since the case was against Shenine, he told her he would have a friend take on the case. So, he asked me to do it."

"He knew these hoes were fucked up so why did he involved you in this shit."

"I said that same thing. He said he wanted someone he knew they couldn't get over on, so he asked me. He told me he was surprised to learn that I got involve with Mari. He never saw that coming because he thought I was as straight as they come. I then told him all this shit that is going on with them and Raq's ass. He said he knew because Raq called him frantically about them stealing the tape with Shenine sucking his dick. Albert said that Raq wanted to give him the heads up about it in case it comes out."

"Shenine is a child, wow!"

"Virgie, that bitch isn't a child. She is 23 and these hoes know exactly what they are doing. Mari lied to get him to do what she wanted. Albert knew about Shenine sucking his dick but remember I told you he said he passed out. Well, they drugged him with something. These hoes dressed his ass up like a woman and supposedly did some strange things to him. That's the shit on the tape that can't get out."

"What? Are you fucking serious?"

"Yes, I am! That's their thing. They didn't know that a camera was in the home recording it all. Albert said he saw the video. It was stored in Raq's cloud but Raq didn't tell me. These hoes want money from Raq and Albert. They are threatening to say Raq put them up to drug Albert and extort him for inside information because of his job. When I tell you I hate these bitches? You just don't know."

"So, tell me how you know Albert has cancer?"

"He said that he would take all of them down one by one, but he was recently diagnosed with cancer and doesn't have the strength to fight them and cancer. I told him that I have Poochie representing me and for him not to worry. I promised him I would get them one by one."

"Wow, I'm so sorry to hear he's sick. We need to develop a real plan to expose their asses for real. They can't continue doing this shit."

"I know, their shit will hit the fan. I promise it will!"

I'm in my car thinking. I can't believe Mari and Shenine. Why do women always try to destroy one another? They have definitely met their match this time. Poochie doesn't play fair. He will destroy them for sure. Don't break the law, fight with the law and then ask the law for help. I'm glad someone is about to stop their asses. As I am thinking about this shit, my sister MJ is calling.

"Hey sister!"

"Virgie Mae, where are you?" I hope that this woman is not about to tell me some more shit that would get me unraveled.

"I'm in the car. I just left Stella's. What's up?" Just say it. They are always wanting to tippy toe around shit.

"I haven't talked to you in a minute. I want to talk to you about Jon."

"Are you home? I will stop by." I am just going to go over there.

"Yeah, I'm here."

"I should be there in about 15 minutes." More than likely I will be there in ten the way I drive.

"Be safe and I will see you soon."

My sister got her a boyfriend. Wow, my sister has a boyfriend. This is crazy. I didn't think it would ever happen. She is pretty hard on men. If she meets a man and he doesn't love the Lord. This woman is running straight out the door just like that.

I arrive early at MJ's and see that Twaab is here too. We haven't done this in a minute. You know hanging out at my grandmother's house talking about boys with Twaab passing judgement because she likes girls.

"Sisters, I'm home."

Twaab says, "this isn't your home. You are stopping by."

"Twaab, leave Virgie Mae alone."

"MJ, I am not thinking about her broke leg ass. I'm home whenever I come here."

"Yeah whatever!"

"Virgie, are you hungry? We were just about to eat."

"Virg, this is her first-time cooking since she had dinner with you and Noble. She has been running around here on the damn phone like a school age girl."

"Aww, my sister has a boyfriend."

"Virg, not for long. She is about to run out of the door on that fine ass doctor."

"What? What happened?"

"What always happens? He is a non-believer."

"Noble said that Jon is going to church with you tomorrow. How is he a non-believer if he is going to church with you?"

"Virgie, he is catholic."

"I'm going to need it to make sense because it doesn't right now. Catholics are believers."

"But I'm Baptist."

"So, you are going to break up with him because he is of another denomination then you. Are you serious?"

"Virg, I said the same thing. She is fucking up this man's head."

"Twaab, stop all that cursing. You sound like Auntie."

"MJ, you haven't even gotten to know him. You are trying to tell me because he is Catholic, so you don't want to get to know him now. I'm all confused."

"I believe what I believe. Can you and Noble come to church too? That's why I was calling you. I don't want him feeling out of place so I thought if you all can come maybe he would be okay."

"Really MJ, you know when I go to church, I lose it. Because of the sinning I do around these parts," as I swipe my hand over my vagina.

"So, I don't know about that. That's why you should go, so you would stop the sinning."

"How does the fact that you have a new boyfriend is your resolution for me to stop committing a sin?"

"Virg, I told her this was not a good idea."

"Please Virgie Mae. I never ask you to do anything, but I am now. Please run it by Noble and let me know later tonight so I can tell Jon."

"Jon is with Noble now. He is probably already telling him."

"Jon isn't with Noble. He was called into the hospital, so they didn't meet." Noble didn't call to tell me that.

We are eating such a delicious meal. We are laughing, talking and putting MJ's outfit together for tomorrow when my phone rings. It's Noble.

"Hey Babe, what time are you coming home? I miss you!"

125

"I came over to MJ's." I need to check his temperature about him not meeting with Jon.

"Did you meet with Jon?"

"No, he cancelled. I was in the house. I ended up calling Laverne's sister." What the fuck? What the hell?

"How is she?" I don't give a damn but I'm going to play along.

"She is good. What time are you coming home? I miss you!"

"Let me wrap up over here and I should be there shortly." Did he just say Laverne's sister? This is crazy, damn! Am I ready for this talk? No, I am not but better now than later.

I have driven so fast to his place. Next thing I know I am entering the condo; Noble did not meet me at the door. He always greets me at the door, so this feels really strange.

"Noble, baby where are you?" There is no answer, so I drop my things on the floor and run into the bedroom. Thank God, he is in the shower. This man scares the hell out of me. I thought he was passed out again or worst. This Laverne shit is fucking with my head. I walked into the bathroom.

"Noble, I'm home."

"Hey Babe, take those clothes off and join me."

"Okay!" I take my clothes off and step into the hot shower. I can definitely use one.

"Let me wash you, relax! I need to check and see that everything I left on you is still there and that damn esthetician didn't change anything."

"Man, cut it out. These hickeys are still right where you left them." He begins to lather the sponge and wash my body as I'm talking. To my surprise, he is really just washing my body. All of this feels so sensual but that's all it is. We are taking turns washing each other while we talk and laugh.

After getting out of the shower, I informed him of MJ's request.

"Babe, I would love to go to church with them."

126

Saturday

"You don't feel out of place there?"

"Why would I feel out of place there? I once heard that the church was a place where all have sinned."

"But. It's one thing to sin. You are constantly sinning. I always feel out of place there when I go."

"Babe, wow! Come here so I can hold you in my arms and make you feel better."

"I'm serious!"

"I am too!" I walk into his arms and he gives me a big hug and kisses my forehead.

"Tell me about the call to Laverne's sister."

"Ever since I saw Sarah last week. She has been on my mind. I called her today because I know Sarah told her I'm back in Chicago." He leads me to the couch as he is talking. "She still has the same number, so I called her. She was pleasantly surprised to be hearing from me. She said she is married and expecting her first child. She still lives in the home I gave her and that her husband is a professional baseball player."

"Is she mad with you? Or blaming you for her sister's death?"

"Della and I have always had a great relationship. She knew I loved her sister to the moon and back and would do anything for her. So, if she is angry with me, she has never expressed it."

"Her name is Della. That's a beautiful name."

"I told her I found someone who makes me happy. She didn't say anything, but I needed her to hear it from me and not Sarah. She told me that she was happy for me but that she misses her sister tremendously. I asked her about how she would have felt that if Laverne was still here and things didn't work out for us. Did she think her sister would want me to find love again? She said no."

I immediately grab his face because I can hear the sadness in his voice. I look into his eyes. He immediately began to cry. This

"Laverne after life shit" is breaking my heart. I don't even know this bitch Della, but she could have lied. Her sister is dead. Why punish Noble because of it? Allow him to live and move forward with his life.

He is lying on the couch as I hold him. He is so broken-hearted by this news. He really loved Laverne. I need to ask myself can he love me this way. Will his heart ache if something happens to me? Will my sisters hold him responsible for the rest of his life? I see why everyone was so worried for him. If I had seen him in this state back then, I would think he would harm himself too. I understand completely. People were fearful of losing him. And I'm sure he was devastated.

SUNDAY

It's 8:14 in the morning. We have slept on this couch all night long. Noble is still sleeping.

I need to call MJ to tell her that we will be coming to church. No, we should surprise her. Listen to me, I don't even know what time it starts I have to call her. I move my arm because it is numb.

"Good morning, babe!"

"Good morning, Noble! How do you feel?"

"I'm good. I don't know what happened there, but I apologize. I know you didn't sign up for this shit. I never wanted to invoke Laverne in our relationship. The crazy part is when Della answered my question, I was numb to her response until I sat here telling you."

He turns to face me and says, "I need this to work. I want this to work. I am willing to put in the time to make it work. I love you! My problem is that I want others to cheer us on. People are not wired like that and that is my problem."

While Noble is in the shower, I should call my Auntie. I know she knows what time church is because she usually attends service with MJ.

"Hey Auntie! I'm calling you because Noble and I are going to surprise MJ at church."

"Really Virgie Mae? I'm going today too with Sid."

"Oh, wow! What time does service starts?"

"Child, at 11. Sid wants to get there early to sit in the back. He calls it the shameful aisle because when the Pastor is preaching everyone back there be looking down. They are ashamed of what they did last night," and she burst out laughing.

"Auntie, where do you sit? Is it back there with Mr. Sid?"

"Hell no, I sit right up front so everyone can see me. I'm too sharp to sit in the back!"

"Well, let me get dressed I will see you soon. Auntie, remember we are surprising MJ?"

"Virgie, when you step in there with that fine ass man. You will be surprising everybody. No one ever thought you would get a man or keep one with your picky ass." Wow, I didn't even know they cared.

Noble and I are dressed heading to church. When we pull up, we can see Jon parking. Noble pulls alongside him and you can honestly see the relief in his face. He is nervous. This must be his first time in a Baptist church or maybe he is nervous because it's my sister's church. Noble is very cool like he attends church all the time. Noble never mentioned attending church before but who am I kidding I don't know what Mr. Noble has done. I am not lying. He keeps me on my toes. He won't even let me stay 10 toes down.

"Hello Jon! Are you good? You look a little nervous there. I can tell you now that the men here love my sister so I would suggest, you man up! Put a stake to your lady. They are about to size you up to see if you are worthy of my sister."

"Thanks Virgie! I don't know why I'm so nervous. I guess because I'm at a church on a date. Or maybe it is because I really like her. We have been on the phone nonstop since dinner. She sends me a morning and evening prayer every day. I don't want to do anything that would mess this up. It's been a long time since I talked or even entertained a woman."

"I can tell you. My sister is a big deal." He better recognize. Kelly's girls are a big deal. Even Dominica if she ever gets and keeps her mind right.

"Jon! What's up man? You got this, no need to be nervous," says Noble. "Thanks, I do have this. Well, we should get inside. Marion is meeting me at the welcoming center."

I know he did not just call MJ "Marion." This is serious and it's just been a couple days.

130

Sunday

Wow! I guess we really do have it like that.

I glance over at Noble. He's holding my hand as we walk into the church. He looks so handsome and strong. As soon as we enter, I see MJ standing next to the desk at the welcoming center. She looks gorgeous. We made sure she brought it today.

MJ's hair is in big curls. We picked out an orange A-line dress and paired it with a bright red waist belt. MJ is wearing a red kitten heel with some beaded bracelets. She even switched her diamond studs for a pair of silver hoops. She's also wearing red lipstick. Noble says that it distracts men to see women in bright red lipstick, so I am the one who encouraged her to wear it. Twaab did her make up. Her face is beat by the gods.

I notice that Jon also sees her, and she sees him too. She lights up like a Christmas tree and walks towards us.

Noble leans into me and says, "Your sister is beautiful!" She definitely is, inside and outside.

Before MJ makes it to us. This older man walks in front of Jon and grabs MJ by the hand leading her in the other direction. It was like something out of a movie. I burst out laughing. She turns to us and tells us to have a seat. Jon is stunned by the ordeal. I then grab his hand to lead him into the sanctuary. When we enter through the door, I scan the congregation for Auntie and Mr. Sid. I immediately observe them sitting in front. We sat down in the back of the church in the "shameful" section.

The service was good. MJ never came to join us. It appeared as if they had her doing a lot of busy work. I felt like they knew she had family there and found things for her to do to keep her from sitting with us.

Jon and Noble seemed to really enjoy the service. I noticed they were actively participating in the "talk to your neighbor, say to your neighbor, and touch your neighbor" call from the pulpit by the Pastor.

We are waiting with Jon so he can speak to MJ before he leaves. Even though I believe I haven't made the best choices in my life, I realize that I am not the only person. The Pastor said in his sermon, "There are those in the church who have not lived up to God's will for their lives. Those who were revealed and those who were not revealed yet." He is not wrong in that statement.

MJ walks over to me and interrupts me in my thoughts.

"Hey sister! Did you enjoy the service?" Before I could answer, Jon interjects.

"Hello beautiful. I really enjoyed the service. Thank you for inviting me and having me accompanied by these amazing guests," pointing to me and Noble.

"Thank you, Jon, I'm so glad to hear it. Would you like to take me to lunch to talk more about it?" Okay MJ, claiming your man in the door in case someone wanted to say something. I'm here for it all.

"I would not have it any other way!" They are too cute with this flirting banter. After Noble and I, they are maybe the next cutest couple out here. They are up here flirting and smiling at each other. I look at Noble with a great big smile. He is smiling the same way. Auntie walks over to Jon then leads him to her friends without even saying a word. She wants to show him off as MJ's boyfriend for bragging rights.

Mr. Sid is standing with us and says, "Virgie, you know Kelle was here too. He said to tell you hello because he had to leave to get to the restaurant." I refused to even look at Noble. I know he is hot.

MJ says, "Mr. Sid, did you meet Mr. Miller? He is the chef here at the church. He could use some advice on his recipes. Auntie told him when you come back to church, she would have you to talk to him." I'm so glad she is leading him away from us. I don't know what else this man was about to say.

Sunday

When they walked away, Noble says, "Babe, why would he come to this church while we are here? He knew we would be here. Did you see him in service? I don't like this at all. His obsession with you isn't healthy for him. I mean that literally. This dude knows how to mess up a day." I knew he wasn't going to take this news lightly. Why the hell would Kelle come to church today of all days? Now when we were dating, he couldn't leave the restaurant for minute. This is some…. you know what I'm not going to think it because we are in church.

"Noble, are you ready to go?" I would like to escape this place. We had such a good service and to hear about Kelle has messed all of that up. Now, I have to hear Noble's mouth about this dude.

"No, let's wait until Jon returns. I don't trust this environment anymore." He is definitely upset by this news.

We waited for Jon to return. We then walked out with him and MJ. I didn't realize it when we pulled up, but Jon drives a Jaguar. No wonder MJ suggested he take her out to lunch that is her favorite car. I wonder if she knew that but knowing her like I do, she did.

Noble is silent on the ride home.

"Do you want to go out to eat?" I have a taste for some fried catfish maybe even some soul food.

"Yeah, let's go to Kelle's! Since he wants to see you so badly. Let's have lunch there." What? Here we go. Really Noble? Kelle is getting under his skin. Wow!

"Really Noble! Why the fuck would we go to Kelle's for lunch? So, you can flex your muscles like you Tarzan and me Jane. Take me home. You and Kelle are too old for this shit. I can't believe I'm cursing after leaving church. You all have me fucked up. Stop using me like I am a piece of meat."

"Babe, what's really fucked up is that I have never used you at all. And to think you are sitting here comparing me to this man, now that's fucked up." We arrive to the condo.

As soon as we step inside, my phone is ringing. Noble is giving me the "is that him" look but it's Twaab. I answer on speaker, so he knows I'm not playing games. I don't have to prove anything to him but after our argument in the car, I felt like this is best.

"Hey sister, what's up?"

"Virgie, I need you to come over to Dominica's. This dude busted her windows out."

I am really going to have to kick Fatel's ass. That is my damn property. I own that damn building. His stupid ass doesn't know that. I told Dominica that the building belongs to my friend and that I'm paying the rent for her. She has no clue I am the friend I talked about.

"Are you serious? Is she okay? I'm on my way!"

"Yeah, she is good. She says she is not leaving though. I called MJ but she told me to call you."

"Okay, she went to lunch with Jon and probably doesn't want to bring him over there. I should be there shortly," and I end the call.

"Babe, do you want me to come with you?"

"No, I will just go. I will be back soon." I think this is the perfect interruption, this conversation was about to be heated. I could feel it. I am driving over to Dominica's when my phone is ringing.

"Hey Natasha Janine! What's up?"

"Girl, I'm trying to get the 411. I heard everybody went to church today. Are you delivert? You know with the "t" at the end."

"Girl you are right. Everybody did come to church even Kelle!"

"I know! I went to the restaurant for breakfast. He told me that he went to church. He said he saw you and your boyfriend."

"I heard he saw us, but we didn't see his ass. Mr. Sid told us after service. Noble is livid about it. That was probably the one time, I wanted to hit Mr. Sid like "you know better, shut your mouth.""

"Kelle said he saw you all immediately, but you all were sitting where he normally sits." I burst out laughing.

"What's funny?"

"Girl, Auntie says that it is the "shameful" section of the church. This suits his ass right with his "shameful" ass!" Now we are both laughing hysterically.

"I'm going to have to call you later. I'm headed to Dominica's because this dude busted out her house windows."

"Okay, be careful. I will talk to you later."

I get to Dominica's house soon after. When I ring the doorbell, this damn fool Fatel answers. Oh, hell no! Why the fuck is he here?

I walk inside of the apartment. Twaab is sitting at the table and Dominica is in the bathroom.

"Twaab, why the fuck is Fatel here?"

"   Virgie, let me explain."

"Don't explain shit to me. I am talking to my sister." I should reach out and touch his ass, but I know the story may not be true so let me get the facts first.

"Sister, he didn't bust the window Dominica did!" Now I should kick her ass. I have to pay for those damn windows.

"What? Please make it make sense." His ass is behind this shit. I know he is.

"Fatel came over to get his stuff when Dominica threw a cup at him and it broke the window. When I got here, she was in here

135

alone, Fatel showed up with some movers to get some more things. They are the ones who told me what happened."

"If he is moving out, why the fuck is he still here answering the door."

"He was on his way out when you rang the doorbell." Dominica comes out the bathroom looking sick.

"Are you okay?"

"This morning sickness started. I can't stop throwing up."

"Well let's get you cleaned up and you can stay at my place because I know you don't want to stay with MJ." I already called maintenance to come board up the window as I was riding over here.

"Thanks sister!"

"Ms. Virgie, can I come to visit her there?" This man is a damn fool. He can't even know my address.

"Hell no, are you fucking crazy? Get your ass out of here!" Twaab is dying laughing.

I drive Dominica to my place. As we are getting off of the elevator, guess who we see.

This bitch Mari with her father walking to the elevator.

"Hello Ms. Kelly," says Mr. Corine. He looks so happy. He really thinks this bitch is so sweet and serene. If he only knew.

"Hello Mr. Corine!" I hate to even speak to him with this bitch by his arm.

"Who is the young lady with you?" This man is nosey as hell but this time I welcome it. He can keep an eye on Dominica in case Fatel brings his ass over here.

"This is my sister Dominica." Dominica is rolling her eyes at him. She hates to see old men flirting with me.

"Hey Mari, you are acting like you don't know who I am," says Dominica.

"Hey Dominica!" This bitch knows Dominica. I should have known. Dominica knows every damn body.

"Hello young lady. I'm Mari's father."

"Aww okay, I thought you were one of those tricks she be fucking around with. Mari makes that money. You still fuck around with Shenine." Mr. Corine is standing here in disbelief. Dominica is telling all of this hoe's business. I am basking in this moment. I'm just standing here so she can keep talking and she does.

"Tell that bitch Shenine, she still owes me some money. I heard y'all was living in this building too. What apartment y'all stay in? So, I can come and hang out. Fatel said his mom kicked her out because she supposedly got grazed by a bullet. You know Ms. Kimble is scary as hell and don't want no one bothering her. I put Fatel ass out too. He is probably back over to his mama's house. He can stay his ass there too. They need each other."

Mr. Corine interrupts and says, "It was nice meeting you, but we are running late for an appointment."

"We didn't really meet. My sister just said your name. Mari makes sure you tell Shenine about my money. I'm going to be staying at my sisters for a minute. Knock on the door. I will come out and kick it with y'all. My sister isn't going to let me have company while I'm over. She likes her privacy and the way y'all be in those streets, we can't trust y'all around her shit."

The whole time Dominica was talking, Mari didn't say a word. She just stood there. I know some of this information is wrong, but Mr. Corine doesn't know that. I'm glad he heard it for himself. I need more information so when we get in the house, I'm all ears.

After we entered the apartment, I ask Dominica, "How do you know Mari and Shenine?" "I met Mari through Shenine. You know Shenine is Fatel's little sister. She is wild. Mari is her girlfriend. Shenine wasn't gay until Mari turned her out. Sister, how do you know those hoes?"

"I don't know them. I met them last week. I heard a lot of disparaging things about them."

"Yeah, they are fucked up! They work at a strip club on the north side. The place is supposed to be a restaurant with burlesque dancers, but they are selling pussy in there."

"Really! I'm curious about this tell me more." Dominica is the type of person who has to be questioned about a topic for her to share its hot gossip.

"Can you get me some crackers to settle my stomach first." I forgot she is pregnant. "Sure!" This is definitely the information we need to stop these hoes. I know there will be some fiction to this story. I will have Poochie, and his investigators figure that out. "Dominica, do you want something to drink?"

"I will have some green tea." Let me hurry up because she will fall asleep in a blink of an eye. She will not remember a thing tomorrow about this conversation.

"Have you ever been to that burlesque dancer's place?"

"No, Fatel and his friend go all the time." How the fuck does he go all the time? He never has any money. Oh, that's probably why. His bitch ass is spending his money at the strip club.

"Sister, you want me to tell you from the beginning?"

"Yeah, because I'm trying to see something."

"I know everything about them hoes. Ms. Kimble, you know Fatel's mom, used to trick off for cash back in her day. She claims she is retired but every time I go over there, there is a new guy. That old bitch is still tricking off. Well, Shenine started doing what she saw her mother doing. She had some guy to pay for her to get some breasts and a bootie job. I wouldn't be surprised if the man who paid for it was someone who was coming over to her mother's house too.

After she had that work done, someone told her about becoming a burlesque dancer to make some fast cash. I call it sophisticated stripping if you ask me. She then got a job at the club where she met Mari. Her and Mari started running tight together and tricking off inside and outside of the club. They would meet a guy in the club then get with him. When they would get with the guy outside of the club, they would steal something valuable of the guys. They would first try to pawn them to get money. But you know pawn shops can't take stolen goods no more, so they started selling them back to the owners. Fatel's friend Tuck is the brain behind that shit with his stupid ass. He fucks with them both, but Mari is the number one girl.

Supposedly, he shot Shenine because she hooked Mari up with a lady. The lady hooked them up with this rich guy. Tuck, goofy ass got mad and shot Shenine in the arm. Fatel's and his cousins are looking for him. Their asses are so scary. They keep playing like they can't find him. Tuck's ass is out west. He isn't hiding from them. Mari's ass has hepatitis which she supposedly got from a customer at the club. She is on disability and getting monthly checks for it. There isn't shit wrong with her. Shenine told me that is part of her scam too. She doesn't have hepatitis. She wants to continue faking like she does to keep getting her government checks." So, this is the shit she doesn't want to get out. I have to tell Noble and Natasha Janine.

"Shenine is so young and dumb. The lady she is listening too is supposed to be her play mother she adopted from the club. Ms. Kimble kicked her out when she came home with her arm in a bandage. That's why I believe Ms. Kimble is still tricking off. She is spooked as hell if she thinks the police may come to her house. She is mad with me right now for calling the police on Fatel for stealing my money. You know they went to her house. She had the nerve to call me and tell me stay my ass away from her. I told her, bitch I will do that with pleasure. Fuck you!"

"Dominica, we are talking about Shenine and Mari."

"Oh, my bad sister, when I think about them it always pisses me off. Like I was saying Shenine met some British lady at the club and started calling her mother. The lady is having them trick off with this rich guy and getting paid, but the guy likes Shenine not Mari. Shenine said that he wants her to leave Mari so he can take care of her. But she won't. Mari is the real fucked up one in their relationship.

When Shenine broke up with Mari, Mari jumped on her at the Willie's nail shop. Willie testified against her but Shenine listened to Mari and changed her story, so Mari got off. Those hoes cannot be trusted. Shenine owes me money. She bought my phone from me then lost it. Remember when I had that iPhone 6, I gave it to her because you bought me a new one. She was supposed to pay me for it, but she didn't. Virgie, I'm tired of talking about these bitches I need to take a nap." She walks to the bathroom and then gets in bed.

I can't believe all this information Dominica has on these hoes. We will destroy these bitches one by one. It's a small world and when you are fucking with people it becomes even smaller. I am going to tell Natasha Janine about this tomorrow. She isn't going to believe me. It all makes sense why the guy Tuck was shooting at Natasha Janine in my building. He must have thought Natasha Janine was the lady who Shenine's is calling her play mother. I couldn't figure out why he was so mad. I wonder if Mari's ass was trying to set her up as the lady. And that's why she asked her to come over to the apartment in the first place. Fatel's ass has all the information. This is probably how Dominica knows so many details. When people don't work, they stay in other people's business.

"Virgie, can you make me another tea?"

"Sure! Sister, who told you all of this?"

"Shenine is the one who tells me this shit. She looks up to me like a big sister. She called me yesterday talking about how her play mother is mad with Mari. Mari supposedly started fucking around with some attorney and fell in love. Shenine said she is fucking up their big pay day, so her mother cut Mari's ass off." She has the nerve to be in love with Natasha Janine. There are tons of lies in that story.

"Just tell me this. How did Mari get a job at Kelle's?"

"I got her that job. She said her dad was tripping about her staying out late. I asked Kelle to hire her for me. You know he loves you so much he will do anything I ask so he did. But he fired her a couple of days ago."

"For what?"

"She was trying to seduce Mr. Sid that's what I heard. My home girl told me that there are two things Kelle doesn't play about Mr. Sid and that pancake recipe. I told my homie she is lucky Kelle fired her because my Auntie would have killed her about her man." Now there is no lie in that. I get Dominica settled in but I'm so tired. I decide to take a nap before I head back to Noble's. I need my energy for what he has planned.

I'm on my way to Noble's. I didn't realize how tired I was. I do not feel like driving into the garage so I will just have the doorman park my car. As I pull up to the front door, I see Sarah, the attorney, get into a cab leaving. Why the fuck would she be at Noble's condo? Was she invited by Noble? Did he contact her? Why would he invite her over here without telling me? This doesn't make sense at all. Yesterday he is on the phone with Della. Today he is meeting with Sarah. I thought after the way he cried last night it would be sometime before we discuss this shit again.

What happened to him saying "he wasn't ready to deal with the whole Laverne ordeal?" I can't wait to get inside. Between him, his damn friend, Natasha Janine, and my family's shit, it's a wonder that I know if I am coming or going.

141

Anthony, the doorman, walks up to the driver side door and says, "Would you like for me to inform Mr. Winston of your arrival?"

"No need, I will be fine. Can you park my car for me," as I get out of the car?

"Please leave the keys at the desk and I will get them later." I hand him $20 as I walk away.

As I am riding this elevator, I'm thinking about how I will reveal this information. I may not have seen her if I had parked my car myself. Noble doesn't know that I saw her get into the cab. Should I immediately tell him what I know? Should I tell him who I just saw leave the building? Should I pretend like I don't know a thing? Should I give him the silent treatment? Well, enough of that. I'm here now so I will do and say what I feel is right.

I am walking to the door when I see Noble opens it. Damn Anthony, you just had to open your mouth.

"Noble, you wanted to meet me at the door."

"Hey babe, I didn't know you were here. I was on my way to the lobby because Attorney McDonald left her glasses on the counter. I didn't want to risk you discovering them and think I was doing some Raq shit."

"Sarah stopped by. I thought I recognized her leaving. What brought her this way?"

"I will tell you when I get back. Let me run the glasses downstairs. I prepared dinner so step inside and settle down. I will be back shortly," he kisses my cheek and runs to the elevator.

When I step into the apartment, I see a large envelope on the table. The lawyer in me, would not allow me to bypass that so I went to check it out.

The envelope is addressed to Noble from the office of Attorney Sarah McDonald and Associates. This must be the letter Laverne left with Sarah. I didn't even know he decided to finally acknowledge the elephant in the room. He could have prepared me for this. Now I'm wondering if the letter isn't something to encourage him to move forward. It could be a letter that is designed to blame him for not coming to her rescue. I think Noble was right. The old relationship is going to affect our relationship. I should have listened but no, I have to encourage him to face his past.

I am just standing at the dining room table when Noble returns.

"Babe, I guess your x-ray vision is either reading the letter word for word or the foil lining inside of it is blocking it. Which one is it?"

"Noble, you didn't mention that you spoke with Sarah. You haven't even said a word about her since last Sunday. I come home, I mean your house and see her leaving. This is very concerning to me. What is going on here? Why all of the side chatter with her and Laverne's sister? And now there is an envelope addressed to you on the table. I don't want to talk about x-ray vision. I want you to tell me what's going on."

"Babe, I know I shouldn't be making light if this. I promise I will explain everything. Let us settle down first then we can talk."

"Not this time! If you love me like you say, then start talking now."

"Sarah called me and said she has an envelope for me. I told her that I didn't want the letter from Laverne. She said that Della called her and informed her that I had called her. Sarah said that Della is bothered by the fact that I have moved on. I told her that she was free to bring the envelope because I am ready to move on. When she gets here, she presents me with this," pointing to the envelope.

"What does it say?"

"I don't know."

I grab the envelope and open it without even asking his permission.

"Noble, Della is suing you for wrongful death of her sister and for control of her estate!" What the fuck just happened?

"She is doing what?" I know he heard what I said but I will repeat it.

"She is suing you for wrongful death and control of her sister's estate."

"How am I responsible for her sister's death?" I want to tell him they believe she killed herself.

"Sarah, called me in the office earlier this week. She said that they think you are covering up Laverne's death."

"Virgie, are you telling me you had a conversation with Sarah about this? And this is your first time mentioning it. Are you fucking serious? What the fuck is wrong with you that you would not tell me? How could you keep something so important to yourself? You have to be fucking lying!"

"I'm not! She called me to warn me of you. Sarah said she been trying to contact you for several years regarding a pressing matter. I told her that she should be speaking with you or your lawyer regarding this matter. But she insisted to tell me. Sarah told me that she has represented Laverne and her family for years. She said that you all started dating in high school and after her death you were devastated. Sarah then said your behavior worried them so that they thought you were lost without her."

"Virgie, but I had told you all that."

"I know but she called me. I didn't reach out to her. You are up here yelling at me when you all are walking around here with all these damn secrets. You should have been honest with me from the start. If anyone should be angry, hell it should be me. I am the one discovering something big on the seventh day of the week. I should be saying to you "what the fuck" and not trying to explain myself."

Sunday

"Babe, you're right I haven't revealed every aspect of my life but when something shows up, I share."

"Really Noble, is that what the fuck you think is sufficient enough? I don't know shit about you, your past, your family, and what makes you tick. What I do know is? You are a mysterious person. You leave me with tons of questions. So, miss me with this bullshit about how I am keeping shit from you."

"You know Virgie, I planned to take you to meet my family." What? Is he serious?

"Yes, I'm serious, I'm ready to deal with my shit. My mother's birthday is next week. I asked my sister and her fiancé to come so you can meet them all." Wow, I'm in shock. He walks up to me, "I don't like how this shit is playing out either. Sarah came over here as a friend to Laverne. She sat here telling me that I need to close this chapter soon and left this envelope. Because she said that, I was under the impression that this was the actual note from Laverne. I would have never imagined that Della would hold me responsible for her sister's death. Not to mention sue me for her estate. I would have gladly given it to her. To be perfectly honest I thought since I didn't claim it and her being next of kin. She would automatically inherit it."

"It doesn't work like that. You are the listed beneficiary and because you are alive and well, it's rightfully yours."

"I'm so angry right now. Why would she even think I had something to do with the death of my first love?"

"Sarah said that Laverne and others believed you were having an affair?"

"What? An affair? I never even looked at another woman. I told you how I was raised. She was the only woman I ever wanted or needed. I can't even fathom why Laverne would say that or think it. I worked countless hours so that she could live the life she wanted. To think, she felt I was unfaithful is bullshit. That

145

information is coming from Della. It has to be. We were immensely happy in our relationship. I don't buy this shit they are selling."

"Sarah said that you had her autopsy sealed after her death. Why did you think you needed to do that?"

"Della wanted the coroner to find out which food or foods caused the allergic reaction. She wanted to file a lawsuit against the company for Laverne's death. I was not going to take Laverne's body through that. I couldn't take any more trauma. I was beside myself with despair, so I had it sealed. It was my decision to make. I told her then that if it was money, she sought I would hand the estate over to her. She refused."

"Sarah said they thought that her death was the result of suicide and that you are covering it. She said that Laverne called Della that night of her death. Della believed that she would do something to harm herself since you were not home to care for her. It was as if Della thought Laverne felt like you abandoned her."

"Babe, what I loved about Laverne was she always saw the beauty in everything. She loved people, to travel, shopping, and me. However, the last couple of months she started to change. She decided one day that we wouldn't eat beef or pork, so we only ate poultry and fish. Then she decided we would not patronize some of our favorite restaurants, so we only ate at local restaurants in Hype Park. The next thing was she didn't want to spend money, so we stopped shopping. The final thing was she said we needed to become vegetarian and that's when I said enough. I told her if that was something, she wanted to do then I would support her, but I was not doing it. Do you see how small I am? I would have withered away."

"So, you purposely worked late because you didn't want to come home?" Noble is sitting here and not saying a word. He is avoiding making eye contact with me.

Sunday

"So Noble, you did abandon her? And that's why you feel so guilty. Aww, you abandoned her!" And, just like that we are both sitting here crying.

He abandoned Laverne. He left her in their home sick with pain and didn't see about her. She probably knew that he wasn't coming. This is why she called him at the hospital. She was trying to get his attention because she felt she was pushing him away. The love of his life was changing before his eyes. She probably didn't know what to do because he had taken care of her for so long. She was dependent on him. He saw that she was unraveling and didn't recognize it. Wow, poor Laverne. She loved this complicated man, but it sounds like she was a complicated woman too.

"Babe, I abandoned her. When she called me at the hospital, my shift was over. I was talking to some doctors joking around when I got the call. I heard her voice and she sounded normal. She started first complaining that I forgot to pick her up some items from the store. She ended up eating some stuff that was already there. She thought that it may been outdated and was making her stomach hurt. I told her to take something for her stomach and lie down. I told her that they needed me to help in the ER and I would be home soon. After I hung up the phone, I told Jon that if he wanted, I would stay and help out."

He went on to say, "So, I stayed. The crazy part was the ER wasn't crowded that day. I just didn't want to hear her nagging and complaining. I wasn't used to that so when I arrived in the house. I noticed that dishes were still in the sink. She was obsessed with a cleaned house. For her to leave dishes behind that was proof to me that she wasn't faking, she wasn't well. So, I rushed into the bedroom and saw her lying in the bed. Her face was swollen and there was no pulse. I started performing chest compressions. She was dead. And from the looks of it, she had been that way for some time. I called the paramedics, her sister and Jon. They all arrived minutes after each other. I abandoned her. I punished myself with this thought for years. I abandoned her, I did. That's why I was so devastated. I felt like it was my fault. I told her to lie down. I should have told her to call the paramedics or had her take a Benadryl. I am a doctor! I know life saving measures."

Noble finishes by saying, "When I was in Italy, I sought therapy. I learned that it was not my fault but every so often I would blame myself all over again. It happened when I saw Sarah. Jon told me that he saw her early that day walking through the ER to the main hospital. He wanted to warn me that I may see her. When we were leaving, I saw her, she was in the gift shop by the entrance. Sarah and Laverne had more than a business relationship, they were friends. Sarah grew up with Laverne and they remain close knit. So, I am very familiar with her because we saw each other often."

"I was wondering why you were not surprised when you saw her talking to me."

"I was surprised that you knew her. I should have guessed you all may know each other since the both of you are lawyers in Chicago. Normally doctors always seem to know other doctors so I figured that would be the same for you all."

"What now Noble?"

"I will have to get an attorney to represent me. I was just about to surprise you with the news that I will be reinstated at the hospital. However, I can't with these kinds of accusations looming over me."

"Aww, babe! Congratulations, I'm so happy for you."

"Yeah, I'm pretty stoked too."

"Do you have any pictures of you and Laverne? I would love to put a face with a name."

"Yeah, we took a picture at this event she threw at our house of all of us." He gets up off of the couch and goes into the bedroom. He returns with a picture in his hand.

"Babe, this is Laverne. She has on the pink dress." I can feel myself about to pass out again.

Laverne is Mikki's "best friend" if you know what I mean. Wow! Does Noble know?

About the Author

S. S. Suggs knows firsthand what sensual encounters can do for romantic relationships. The author is well sought after for relationship advice and ideas for exchanges of intimacy. S. S. Suggs is a graduate with a bachelor's degree in Sociology (the study of human behavior) and a master's degree in Arts and Science.

S. S. Suggs is a storyteller who enjoys exploring the imagery of sensual encounters, bringing sensual encounters to life through her words. As expressed in volume one, the readers became captivated by the story of Virgie and Noble as they journeyed together daily loving each other differently. It is with a background in human behavior and arts and sciences, the author uses her education to help people through the complexity of relationships. With a love for details and descriptive language, the author takes an approach on word play to audiences from all backgrounds.

Epilogue

A sensual conversation that has had its fair share of adventure. Will Virgie tell Noble what she knows? Does Noble know about Laverne? How will Virgie react? We must learn more about these lovebirds. Even though they are different, it appears they are so much alike.